"Listen, son," Tom Davisson said. "You believe a thing or you don't. You start making exceptions and you head into trouble. This is a rough country out here. We're trying to get some law established because that's the only way most people can get along together. I say I'm the law but I'm only part of it. Somebody steps out of line and it's my job to get him and turn him over to the court to decide is he guilty and what should happen to him."

"This one's guilty," I said.

"Sure," Tom said. "Guilty as hell. But it's not my job to say that or what to do with him."

"When your law hangs him," I said, "he won't be any deader than if he was swung yesterday."

"But the whole job'll have been done right," Tom said.

FIRST BLOOD
by Jack Schaefer

Also by Jack Schaefer

SHANE

Jack Schaefer

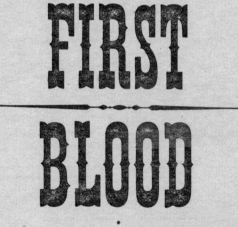

FIRST

BLOOD

And Other Stories

BANTAM BOOKS

TORONTO • NEW YORK • LONDON • SYDNEY • AUCKLAND

FIRST BLOOD AND OTHER STORIES
A Bantam Book / published by arrangement with the author

PRINTING HISTORY
Bantam edition / February 1988

Bantam Books are published by Bantam Books, a division of Bantam Dou-
bleday Dell Publishing Group, Inc. Its trademark, consisting of the words
"Bantam Books" and the portrayal of a rooster, is Registered in U.S. Patent
and Trademark Office and in other countries. Marca Registrada, Bantam
Books, 666 Fifth Avenue, New York, New York 10103

Contents

Introduction

First Blood, first published in book form thirty-five years ago, is the novel which settled me into a free-lance writing career—and at the same time really began my education in the often weird and sometimes wonderful things that can happen to a manuscript once it has left its author's typewriter.

I had already written plenty of words as a long-time working newspaperman. Back along the way, while still doing daily newspaper chores, I had experimented with a short novel that had finally been published in late 1949 under the title *Shane* and was showing signs of doing moderately well. But rarely can a would-be writer establish a career on the basis of one book. And now (this was 1951), no longer working as a journalist, I had already had a go at the traditional high hurdle—the attempt at a second book—and had failed that test completely.

Shane, by definition, was a "western." Through college and into graduate school I had been a classics major leading on into English literature. After the publication of *Shane*, well-meaning friends had been constantly telling me that it was all very well to want to write books, but did they have to be "westerns", those potboilers low on the totem pole of literary critical esteem? I had tried to argue that there was no reason why a writer could not at least try to create literature about the "West" as about the "East" or the "South" or the "big city", or for that matter about any area and/or time in the history of mankind—and that western American history had become my current major interest anyway. Oh, no, no, no, had been the persistent advice; anything but a "western."

And so-o-o . . . I tried writing an "eastern."

That had been hard work, work I had to push myself into daily, but I had plugged along and finished it. As I recall, it was not so bad. Obviously not so good either, because no one wanted to publish it. The high hurdle had tripped me neatly. Discouragement was setting in. And then I had remembered something possibly significant. About halfway through that "eastern" struggle, I had, for some reason I have never quite fully fathomed, taken a few days time-out to write a short story, a rather bitter and tragic short story about a sheepherder in Wyoming territory. Definitely a "western." And the editor of a national magazine had promptly accepted it.

During the next few months I tried myself out with a few more short stories, each a "western" and each promptly sold. I felt I might be ready to try that high hurdle once again.

This time, primed by much reading and research, emphasis on stagecoach travel in the early days of the Far West, I began talking in my own mind to a young man named Jess Harker. Eventually I persuaded him to start telling his tale. And to continue with it. And to finish it. Not all by quite a margin what I had hoped it would be—but at least complete with a beginning and a middle and an end. I sent the manuscript to a literary agent and sat back to wait. Only a few weeks and word came. Houghton Mifflin, which had published *Shane*, would do this one, too. Then the fiction editor of *Collier's* magazine decided the story might do as a three-part serial prior to book publication. A good, a very good beginning. And then . . .

A title was needed. My choice from the beginning of the writing had been and still was *Solstice*, the term for the marking of a change of season, weatherwise the shift into summer or the shift into winter, in the case of my story a change of season in the life of young Jess Harker. But no, insisted Houghton Mifflin. Not enough direct appeal to inveterate readers of "westerns." Not sufficient suggestion of violence and gunfire and gore. *First Blood* should do nicely.

I objected, I argued, I complained that use of the numerical term "first" would suggest that my decent and basically law-abiding Jess was really the kind of Billy the Kid gun-toter who would quite likely go on to second and third and perhaps even fourth and fifth "bloods." But of course, as only a beginner in the free-lance writing field, I could not (or certainly thought I could not) do much insisting on my own. The book title became and ever since has remained *First Blood*.

Meanwhile the editor at *Collier's* had decided for himself on yet another title. He noted a pointed and somewhat symbolic reference in the story to a "black rawhide whip with a stock that had hand-worn silver decorations on it." His choice became *The Silver Whip*. To some extent, to my mind, this was something of an improvement. Then, somewhere along the editorial line a decision was made to trim the text down from three to two installments. Whoever did the actual trimming had a heavy hand. *Collier's* used *The Silver Whip* as the title, all right—but any reasonably careful reader could note that there was not a single reference to a silver whip anywhere in the trimmed text. (I do have a vague recollection that there was something that could have been a silver-handled whip in one of the illustrations.)

And then again . . .

On the strength of those two installments, well before the book itself would appear, 20th Century-Fox offered to buy film rights. Young people at the studio, a group that might be called a new generation of filmmakers, some of them the sons (and perhaps the daughters, too) of long-time studio people, including the son of overall bigwig Darryl Zanuck himself, wanted to try some filmmaking ideas of and on their own and thought that the silver-whipless *Silver Whip* would be a good story with which to start.

A contract was signed. Jesse L. Lasky, Jr., wrote a screenplay, a good screenplay. From my point of view a very good screenplay. Not one designed for a lavish, big scale, overdone John Wayne-type epic. No. For a simple honest straightforward filmic telling of Jess Harker's tale.

Then casting. Those I remember now were young Robert

Wagner as Jess himself, Rory Calhoun as sheriff Tom Davisson, Dale Robertson as Race Crim. Filming got under way and was going along nicely. And then again . . .

As was explained to me later, wht happened then was that Zanuck senior decided to check over what was being done by his studio young ones. He checked all right. And issued a series of recommendations—which, of course, had the practical effect of orders. I cite just one, typical of the thinking behind them all.

Now, the bite in Jess Harker's story, the focal point, virtually the very meaning of it, depends upon the fact that, in the showdown climax, when Jess pulls the trigger of the gun in his hands, Race Crim is killed. The gist of what Zanuck senior recommended on that point was: *Dale Robertson is a popular and upcoming young actor; the ladies in particular like him; they won't like having him killed; have him merely wounded and then recover.*

Now, at this late date, looking back, I am willing to concede that perhaps, in terms of studio economics and actors' contracts, and the constant necessity of turning out reels of finished film, Zanuck senior might have been right. But from my point of view what might have been a crisp and incisive treatment of the ideas imbedded in the story became just another run-of-the-studio-mill film, just another rather routine "western."

Oh, well. While that was going on out in Hollywood, something interesting was developing in regard to book publication.

In those days the usual book was published first as a hardcover with both publisher and author hoping that not only would it do well in that form, but also that, after the usual year's clearance, some paperback publisher would buy the subsidiary rights for its own edition. The catch there, at least from the writer's point of view, was that the paperback royalty had to be split with the original hardcover publisher—and that royalty was a mere four percent. The average paperback sold for a quarter. That figured to a one cent royalty. To be split in half. One half cent.

But better days seemed to be dawning. Ian Ballantine, launching his new Ballantine Books, had recently worked out with Houghton Mifflin a plan for simultaneous hardcover and paperback publication of selected books. The production economies to be achieved would mean that a royalty on the paperback could be at least five percent and possibly as much as eight. With no splitting. Direct to the author. And one of the first two books selected to test the plan was *First Blood*.

That, I insist, was a good idea. And it worked for a time. Then Ballantine Books ran into distribution difficulties, the most troublesome aspect of paperback publishing, and the simultaneous publication plan quietly faded out of existence. But by that time *First Blood* was well launched in this country, had jumped the ocean to do very well in England, and was heading for translation into various foreign languages. I was reasonably certain I had cleared that high hurdle at last and was working on a third and a fourth book.

And now, in 1988, the forever young though season-changing Jess Harker and my aging self are appreciative of the fact that the editors at Bantam Books, who took over paperback publication of *First Blood* after the original fade-out and kept the book in print for a number of years and printings, are issuing it once again. And for myself, I have long ago accepted that *First Blood* title.

—Jack Schaefer
Santa Fe

FIRST

BLOOD

When I brought the stage into Goshen that day I was feeling sorry for myself. It was only a twelve-mile run from the Gap but even so I had to nurse the horses along or they never would make the last climb to the level stretch into town. They were like everything else I had to work with. Old. Maybe they'd been good horses in their time. Their time was past.

The coach was the same. One of the early Concords shoved away years before in some storage barn and pulled out again for this makeshift mail run. Not worth a new paint job and not having it. You could hear the creaking a mile off.

Uncle Ben Nunan was the same again. He was a joke, riding messenger on the seat beside me. So old he could hardly heft the shotgun. The Company kept him on because he'd been with them from the days their first wheels rolled. They had him on this silly sideline run so he could think he was still doing something. He wasn't. He was just along for the ride and because the government said every mail coach had to carry a guard. That was waste weight on this coach. No one would ever have thought of stopping it. We didn't average a passenger a week and our mail pouch was empty most of the time. The Company had added this spur off the main line over to the Gap to please some official in Washington and hold their mail contract. They were hoping to drop it soon.

So there I was sitting beside an old coot who'd have fallen off the box if he had to fire his shotgun and driving a decrepit old four-horse coach that could hardly hold together. And me edging past twenty and full of bounce and knowing I was good. I'd taken care of myself since I was fourteen. I'd had a dozen different jobs and held them as long as I wanted and left only because I liked moving on. I could handle anything on wheels. I could drive anything leather would hold. I'd kept my wagon rolling with a train freighting military supplies into the hills. I'd ridden wheeler with a jerkline outfit. I'd driven a twenty-mule team on the salt flats. I could get as much out of a fast-trotting six-horse pull as any man ever held reins. When I signed with the Company I thought I'd be stepping out. Instead I was plugging along with four old horses so gone they'd have wheezed just standing around in pasture.

They made it up that last rise because I coaxed the effort out of them. We plodded along the level. I looked sidewise at Uncle Ben. He was the only thing around to talk to. "Fine company we work for," I said. "Why in hell don't they give me a good run?"

He flicked a quick glance at me and stared at the road again. The rest of him was almighty old but his eyes weren't. "Maybe," he said. "Maybe they don't think you're ready. Not old enough."

"I'm better'n twenty," I said. "That's grown-up age in this country."

"Wasn't thinking of years," he said.

"What in hell were you thinking of?" I said. "I've got my growth. I was driving for McCardell before I was nineteen."

"McCardell," he said. "A two-stage outfit. Went broke, didn't he? This one's different. Big. Solid. Got a name to keep up."

"Fine way to keep it up," I said. "Putting a driver like me on a pokey hitch like this. First thing they know I'll be quitting. I can handle horses, can't I?"

"Yes," he said. "Yes. You can handle horses." He flicked that quick glance at me again. "Can you handle yourself? Take a job and hold it? Take the ribbons on a main-line run and remember every mile what's in the coach is more important than you and your opinion of yourself?"

That was the way it was. I couldn't even talk to him much. He was too old to see things my way.

We plodded along the level and Goshen began to take shape ahead. "Jess," he said, "don't fight the bit, boy. Maybe you've got the makings. You just ain't made yet."

"Shut up," I said. "I like me the way I am." We were about a half-mile out of town and I was peeved at him and that excuse for a job I was doing. I shook out my whip and snapped the tip by the lead team's ears. They perked a bit and tried to set a trot and inside of a hundred feet they were plodding at a walk again. I was mad then and I thought to hell with the rules and I laid the leather to them. They smacked into the traces and stumbled into a fast trot and the wheelers caught it and we lurched along the road at almost a good clip. We hit the main street and swung over toward the station and I leaned my weight on the brake and pulled hard on the lines, and we stopped swaying by the station porch. Uncle Ben let loose of the handrail and looked at me and shook his head a little. He eased himself down and reached back for the mail pouch and went up on the porch and through the right-hand door to the waiting room. I called out for the stock tender and jumped down and went around the coach and up on the porch and I saw Luke Bowen standing in the left-hand doorway, the one to his office. He was division superintendent, the man who'd hired me. He didn't say anything. He just came to the porch edge and stood there looking at the horses. Sweat was working out into a lather on them and their legs were trembling.

"That what you want?" I said. "A good showing? That's the way I hear you want it along the line. Drag it in the open if you have to but swing it fast for a good showing at the stations."

"Not on your run," he said. "And you know it." He looked ready to lace into me and I was ready to flare back. But he turned and went into his office and stopped for a moment in the doorway. "Knock the little that's left out of those horses and you'll be looking for another job."

I thought of some good answers for that but I'd have had to follow him in to say them. I scuffed at the porch and stepped down and started up the street. I didn't even bother to go into the waiting room and sign the manifest. Uncle

Ben would take care of that. He liked to putter around with the paperwork. I went on up the street and turned into the Hatt House for a drink and right away I began to feel better. Frank Hatt had pushed his bartender aside and was tending his bar himself and he had reason for that. Maybe a dozen were strung along it and in the middle of them, leaning back and holding a glass up to see the whiskey color clear, was Race Crim.

It's hard to put into words how I felt about Race Crim. He was the kind of man I wanted to be and knew I couldn't ever be. I didn't have the size and the looks. I didn't have the dash and the color and the ready tongue and the easy assurance that could make most everyone a friend or the hard core of reckless courage underneath. He was big and handsome and he could forget all the rules and the Company would never fire him because he was the top messenger along the whole main line. No one stopped a stage when he was on the box. He was wicked with a gun, rifle or revolver or shotgun the same. There were tales about him all through the territory. Like the time he took his coach through four miles of running Indian raid and when they retraced the route afterwards they found the bodies of seven braves along the way. And the time a couple of road agents tried to bushwack him and he made the driver stop the coach and he jumped down and shot it out, and with a bullet hole in his own left arm helped lug their bodies in.

He was older than me, fifteen years or more, but he wasn't so old he couldn't see things the way a young one like me did. People always crowded around where he was and he'd let me be one of them and talk to me like I was one of the old-hand drivers and sometimes because I worked for the Company too he'd even act like we sort of shared a little something extra between us. He was there by the bar now, tall and broad in his Company outfit, and just the sight of him made me feel better.

He saw me coming through the doorway. He sank his drink and set the glass on the bar. "Jess," he said, "come over and toss one down with me. These town folk are all right in their way, but they don't really know how a stage-faring man feels. Something like vegetables. Rooted in one place."

"Glad to, Race," I said, going over and trying to walk

the way he did, rolling my shoulders just a bit and coming off my heels with a little spring. "If you let me pay the ante."

"Got here first," he said. "That means I hog the honors." He told Frank Hatt to hand drinks around and then lifted his. "It'd pleasure me, boys," he said, "to have you drink to my record. Never had a coach stopped. Never intend to."

I downed mine and liked the feel of it roughing my throat. "Damn right," I said. "Only a fool'd try."

He grinned at me and poked me in the ribs. "Appreciate me, eh, Jess? Good boy. Has Bowen still got you buried on that spur to the Gap?"

"Yes," I said. "I'm about ready to quit."

"Don't blame you," he said. "A boy like you's worth more than that. One of these days I'm going to tell him so."

"You will, Race?" I said. "You will?"

"Sure, Jess," he said. "Sure. One of these days." He took my glass and set it with his on the bar for refills. We were lifting them when a voice from the doorway stopped us. "Take it easy, Race. Jess likes the stuff enough without you encouraging him." We turned and Tom Davisson was there watching us.

It's even harder to tell how I felt about Tom Davisson. That went way back, way back when I was about fifteen and thinking maybe I'd be a ranch hand and get to be good and make a name at the rodeos. I was getting a cot and keep as handyman around a livery stable and I had my first horse, a one-eyed old cow pony nobody else wanted. I'd been practicing with a rope, and one day I rode out into the open country and found a steer wandering off by his lonesome. Just to see if I could do it I kept throwing till I had a loop over his horns and head. We were in a fair state by then, me and the horse, and there we were with the steer stiff-legged and mad at one end of the rope and us at the other, and I was beginning to realize I'd got us into a fix. I couldn't get the rope off without dismounting and loosening it and pulling it over the horns and being on the ground with that steer would be a mighty dangerous proceeding. I was so intent on that problem that I nearly jumped out of the saddle when I heard a voice behind me. "What the devil you doing with a rope on another man's cow?" I swung in the saddle and there was this man, medium-sized and stocky and along somewhere in his mid-forties, sitting easy and quiet on a big black horse. He had a capable-looking gun hanging at his right hip and his right hand was hooked in his belt close by it and his face was hard and stern under his hat brim. "Speak up," he said. "Make it good. I'm Tom Davisson."

I knew the name. He was a range detective for the local cattleman's association and I'd heard talk about him. What I'd heard didn't help me feel good right then. He was said to be as tough as weathered hickory on anyone who stepped outside the law or even took to stretching it a bit. I started telling him who I was and how I was only trying to learn to use a rope and I was getting more worried with every word till I saw that his eyes weren't hard like his face. He reached up the hand that had been hooked in his belt and pushed his hat back.

"Well, son," he said, "you got your rope on that critter. How you going to get it off?"

I didn't know and said so. He chuckled and shook out his own rope and rode around behind the steer and dropped his loop on the ground and when the steer moved quartering away and stepped in the loop he pulled it tight around the back legs. While he held the steer I dismounted and freed my rope and hopped back in the saddle and started coiling it. Before I was half through he had shook slack into his own rope, let the steer step out of it, and had it coiled and hung on his saddle. "Son," he said, "maybe you've learned something. Never put your rope on another man's property."

That was the first time I saw him and after that he'd pop up so often wherever I was, and I moved around plenty, that finally it got through to me he was sort of keeping an eye on me. Maybe that was because he knew I didn't have any folks. Others knew that too but they didn't have the same kind of bump of responsibility. His was a big one and he had a habit of being around when things were happening with me. Like the time I got mad and quit at the livery stable and he told me about the job with the freighting outfit. That was when I found my hands were made right for reins and I learned what it was to have the tingle of good horses coming through them. And he was the one told me after McCardell went broke that Bowen might give me a place. But he had another habit that had been getting on my nerves. He had to be giving me advice all the time. Maybe that was because he'd been a law man of one kind or another all his life and spent so much time watching that people did things right and stuck to regulations. But he was sheriff of the district now with headquarters in Goshen and that was too close for my comfort. I didn't want him around jawing me when I stepped out for a little fun and telling me what I ought to do. I wanted to live my own life my own way. I guess I knew deep down I'd never get away from the warm feeling that ran through me when I was stuck with that steer and I saw that no matter how hard his face was his eyes were different. But I couldn't feel about him like I did about Race Crim. I respected Tom Davisson and was grateful to him when I stopped to think about it, which wasn't too often. But I admired Race Crim and was proud to be seen in his company.

And here we were, the three of us, the two of them crossing looks over me in the barroom of the Hatt House. And that was bad because they were both men people thought a lot of and they'd known each other a long time and been in tight spots together when posses were riding. Then Race was grinning. "Take it easy yourself, Tom. Get human for a change. Come on and have a snifter with us."

Tom Davisson didn't grin back. He shook his head. He spoke slow and thoughtful. "I'd hate to have to tangle with you, Race, over the boy."

Race kept right on grinning. "Tangle with me, Tom? You and me aren't going to tangle over anything. Not ever. Not you. Not me." He tossed down his drink and I took my cue and did the same. "Forget it, Tom," Race said. "Why not let Jess decide for himself? He's full grown."

"Damn right," I said. "I can handle myself. I'll do things my way."

Tom Davisson shook his head again and looked at us and turned suddenly and faded out of the doorway. Race aimed his grin at me and poked me in the ribs. He kind of shoved the whole business aside with a wave of his hand and started telling us there at the bar one I'd never heard before—about the time he was on the box with Russ Thorp driving and they had some thousands in bullion aboard. A bunch of sharpers, they never knew just who, had dropped a tree across the road and he and Thorp never slowed but swung off through the brush, jolting all over the landscape, and ran smack into the bunch hunkered down in the bushes, and blasted their way through and got back on the road and pushed on without the wheels ever stopping once. "That was no time to do any checking," he said. "Must have been half a dozen in that brush popping at us. Can't be certain but think I winged a few."

That was Race Crim. I'd have shucked ten years of my life to be driving beside him. We were standing there saying what came to mind about that story when someone spoke up different. "What you doing all decked out today, Race? Your regular run don't start till tomorrow." I looked at him and he was that strange duck, a sallow-faced any-aged one, who had been around town several weeks hanging out a lot at the station and buying drinks for any of us stagers would talk to him. He'd said he was thinking of starting some business but he hadn't said what kind.

Race didn't pay any particular attention to him. Race was thinking about that story of his and feeling good and liking to hear his own words. "Well, now," Race said, shoving his glass along the bar for a refill. "You all know how it is. When the Company's got something special moving they send for me."

"Something special?" said this man, sliding the words out soft and casual.

Race saw him then. It seemed to me Race looked a mite worried for a second. "Sure," he said. "But not too special. Sort of a trial run trying to clip some time off the schedule. Bowen's a bear on making time. They want me aboard just to make it look good." He took his glass and started fiddling with it, sloshing the whiskey around and watching it.

"Who's driving?" I said.

Race looked at me and suddenly it wasn't such a friendly look. "Thorp," he said, short and dry.

"That's funny," I said. "I guess Russ Thorp's about as steady a driver as there is. But he ain't one for making fast time."

Race looked at me like he wished I'd shut up. He poked me in the ribs and maybe that seemed friendly to the others but it didn't feel friendly to me. "Listen to him," he said. "Listen to this kid here. Talks like he thinks he could run a stageline better'n Bowen, who was doing it proper before this pup here was weaned." The others were beginning to chuckle. He'd turned it on me all right. He leaned over and poked me again. "Why, I'll bet, Jess. I'll bet you think you ought to be up on that stage this afternoon snapping a whip and trying to act like a grown man." He leaned back laughing and the others followed his lead and I could feel the blood burning my face. I couldn't understand why he'd swung around like that and then I didn't want to understand. I was too mad.

I turned and went out of the place and I was too mad to do more than just notice that the sallow-faced man had slipped out ahead of me and was heading up the street and turning into the livery stable. I went on up the street myself and was thinking I was through around there. I'd quit. I'd show Race and Bowen and the whole passel of them around Goshen. Tom Davisson too. I'd head on north to the gold creeks and make a strike and buy a whole stageline for myself. Or maybe I'd head for one of the really big lines and make them give me a job and get a name as a driver that the Company'd hear about and offer me double pay to come back and take their best run. I'd do something like that. But there was one thing I had to have straight before I left town. I'd been meaning to do it but never quite managed to work up the nerve. Now I was riled enough to try anything.

I slowed my steps and by the time I reached Bentley's Harness Shop I had my words ready in my mind. I went in and Calvin Bentley was where he usually was, cross-legged on a bench, sewing away on a saddle, and Mary Ella was where she usually was, perched on the counter reading a book. She read a lot of books. But she came by that natural. Calvin Bentley had been a schoolteacher for a while back east somewhere before he had to come out to our part of the country for his health. And reading books didn't stop her being a neat and spicy package of a girl. She didn't have the kind of looks to make you stop and forget your manners and stare for a close inspection the first time you saw her. Still, she was easy on your eyes and she wore well and the better you knew her the nicer she was.

"Mister Bentley," I said, "I want to speak to your daughter alone."

"Greetings and salutations, my boy," he said, beginning to wind me up in words the way he always did. "You do not seem your usual chipper self this fine noontime. Alone, you say? With Mary Ella? Young men have the most amazing fondness for being alone with young women. Yet it was the same in my own salad days. Even so youth should step aside for age. I am comfortable here and my tools are handy. If you have things to speak to her not for a father's ears, you must take her outside or into a back room."

Mary Ella had closed her book and slid off the counter and was watching me. I took her by the arm and marched her into the room behind the shop and closed the door and I let go of her arm and planked myself about six feet away so I wouldn't be trying to take hold of her.

"Mary Ella," I said, "you keep quiet till I say what I have to say." I pulled in a big breath and I stuck out my chin and I started talking. "You know how I feel about you. You women always do. You know if I ever get married it's you I want to be married to. Well. I'm fed up with things around this town and the way the Company don't appreciate me—"

"Doesn't appreciate you," she said.

"Doesn't or don't, the meaning's the same," I said. "Well, I'm quitting. I'm leaving for places where people will appreciate me. I've got a little money saved for a stake. There's a man named McCardell managing a new stageline up in Idaho and he knows me. Maybe it ain't so big, but I'll bet it can use a good driver. I'm going up there and he'll give me a job, and anybody can drive the way I can'll get along fine. I'll bet it won't be long before I'm a partner in that line. Well, I want to know, will you marry me and go up there with me?"

Mary Ella never played around with words like her father. She said what she had to say right out. "No," she said, "I won't."

I didn't have much breath left. All I got out was: "I thought you liked me."

"I like you, Jess," she said. "Perhaps I more than like you. I have a hankering to be close to you the way you seem to have about me. But I won't marry you and go off anywhere with you. I don't want a hop-skip-and-jump husband. How long have you been with the Company, Jess?"

"A hell of a long time," I said. "All of three months and I'm still—"

"How many jobs did you have before that?"

"A hell of a lot of them," I said. "And I wasn't ever fired—"

"See?" she said.

"No, I don't see," I said. "I suppose if I was to keep on

driving half-dead horses over to the Gap one day and back
the next for maybe three-four years till somebody died and
the Company maybe might just have sense enough to give
me his run, why then you'd think maybe I ought to be grateful and I'd be all right for a husband."

She pulled her eyebrows down and crinkled her nose like
she did when she was real serious. "I don't know," she said.
"I'm not sure that would make any difference. It's not just
jobs and things like that so much. But a girl like me has to
have a feeling of security in her husband. She has to feel
she can depend—"

There she was, lighting into me the way everybody was.
I was at least a year older than she was and there she was
acting like I was just a young one. I pushed in with my
words. "A planted-vegetable kind of a husband," I said.
"That's what you want. Well. You'll have to find somebody
else then." I went to the door and took hold of the handle.

"Jess," she said. I stopped still and waited and she did
too; then she spoke very soft. "Don't go too far, I won't be
finding anyone else. Not for a long while anyway."

"That's fine," I said. "That's just fine." The way I said
it she knew I didn't mean that at all. I yanked the door open
and went out through the shop.

Calvin Bentley looked up. "Then the lover," he said,
"sighing like furnace—"

"Shut up," I said and went out into the street. I was
through. I was through with the whole bunch of them, with
everything and everybody all around. I pushed along not
caring where I was going, and I was pushing along like that
when somebody came alongside and grabbed my arm and I
swung my head and it was Tom Davisson. "Bowen wants to
see you. Better hurry it."

"Let go my arm," I said. He held on and shook me a little
and I chopped down with my other arm to make him let go
and he stepped back and pivoted to get better leverage and
smacked me along the head so hard I went off the plank
sidewalk and on my rump in the dust of the street. If it had
been anyone else I'd have piled up and into him and maybe
taken a beating but done some damage taking it. But I
couldn't do that. Not to Tom Davisson. Not even though I
was through with him too. I sprawled in the dust and looked
up at him and he stood spraddle-legged and looked down at

me. "Somebody's got to knock sense into you sometime," he said. "Might as well be me. Did you hear me say Bowen wants to see you?"

"Yes," I said. I scrambled up and knocked some of the dust off me. "And the only reason I'll let him see me is because I want to see him. I'm through with his goddam graveyard run. I'm quitting."

I started off expecting to hear a lecture following, but all I heard was a queer sound and I had to look back. Tom Davisson's face was hard as it always was but I could tell the sound was a chuckle deep in his throat. I was too mad to try to figure that. I headed straight for the station and went up on the porch and through the door of Bowen's office with my mouth all set to say what was in my mind and I stopped short just inside and didn't say a thing. Bowen was sitting behind his desk chewing on a pencil. Race Crim was leaning, big and handsome and nodding at me like he never had turned on me at all, against the left wall. Billy Skinner, another of the messengers, was sitting on one edge of the desk. In the right rear corner on a chair was Uncle Ben Nunan. I could tell plain as if I'd bumped into a stone wall something big was going on in there and me and my peeve might seem something small to them.

"Close the door," Bowen said around the pencil. I closed it and he took the pencil out of his mouth and pointed it at me. "Jess. Think you could take the main stage the whole first leg from here down to Stillwater where the next driver'll pick it up?"

I couldn't do more than gulp at him. It was that sudden. He was impatient and started tapping with the pencil. "Russ Thorp's been took sick. The doc says blown his appendix or something like that. Anyways he can't drive. Can you take his place?"

I had it then. I rocked a little on my toes and hooked my thumbs in my belt the way I'd seen Race do many a time. "Quit fretting, Luke," I said. "You're damn right I can."

Bowen looked at the pencil and set it carefully on the desk top. He stretched up out of his chair and kicked at a desk leg. "See what I mean?" he said to the others. "I won't buy it even if Tom does say it might do. The kid's not seasoned. And I don't like his attitude. We'd better wait. I've telegraphed down the line and another driver can make it here by four if I give the word. That'd only make us about three hours late."

No one said anything and then it was Uncle Ben back in the corner who spoke, quiet and mild. "The boy's all right. Give him his chance."

Bowen sat down slow and picked up the pencil and stuck it in his mouth again. He chewed on it thoughtful for maybe a full minute. "Let it ride," he said. "The kid's driving."

I never felt better in my life. I knew that when Luke Bowen made up his mind nothing short of a dynamite blast could budge him. And I thought I knew what had been bothering him. "I'll show you what I can do," I said. "I hear you're wanting to make time this trip. I'm the cookie can do that for you."

Bowen's mouth dropped open and the pencil fell to his lap and bounced to the floor. "Make time?" he said. "Listen, kid. I'll be satisfied if you come even just fairly close to staying to schedule. What we're after this trip is getting through without any trouble. Nothing else and no fancy business." He leaned forward over the desk and spoke low in a voice that had me tingling down to my boots. "You'll be carrying the biggest batch of bullion we've had on the line in five years or more. Twenty-seven thousand dollars worth. They've cleaned a good pocket over at the mines and this is it. There'll be no trouble unless you make some. Even Ferguson who's shipping it doesn't know it's moving today. No one knows but just us here in this room."

Race Crim moved over by the wall. "And Thorp," he said.

"The same thing," Bowen said. "Thorp's steady. He never talks."

"Davisson too," Billy Skinner said. "But that's more of the same."

The sun outside was already shading past noon and the coach was to leave at one. I stayed in the office pretending to listen to Bowen telling me how to take the run. But I wasn't listening. I was walking around high in the clouds somewhere, rolling my shoulders just that bit and coming off my heels with that little spring, and people were watching me and pointing me out and claiming to each other they knew me and were friends of mine. I didn't need to listen anyway. I knew every stop and swing station from Goshen to Stillwater and beyond as well as if I'd been driving the road myself. I'd talked every chance I could to every driver who'd let me ever since I was with the Company.

We had sandwiches and coffee in the office that Uncle Ben brought from the waiting room and then he ducked out of sight somewhere while we began to get ready. The Company liked to dress its men and Bowen found me one of the jackets, tough corduroy trimmed with velvet. He couldn't find a pair of the pants but I already had the boots and one of the broad-brimmed hats, so with the jacket I was near enough complete. Billy Skinner grunted at me in it and dropped a Colt in the right side pocket of his own jacket and filled the left side pocket with extra shells for his shotgun. Race buckled a second gunbelt around his waist so he had two Colts riding below his hips under his jacket, and picked a Spencer repeater out of the wall rack. We were ready to step out on the porch and whistle the coach from the stable when I had a bad moment. I didn't have a decent whip.

Nothing meant more to a driver in those days than his whip. For a six-horse drag he needed a nine-foot rawhide lash on a sturdy packed stock. He didn't use it on the horses themselves unless that was absolutely necessary or he was raw young and feeling mean the way I was coming over from the Gap that morning. He used it to tell them what he wanted by the different sounds he could make snapping it past their ears. Matter of fact, if he was a good driver he didn't need it at all. He talked to them through the reins. But the whip was the sign of his trade, his badge, and if he couldn't flick a fly off a lead horse's rump without touching the skin while swinging along at a fast trot he didn't deserve to have one. I had one, a good one that Calvin Bentley made for Mary Ella to give me my last birthday. But it was over at the Gap. I wouldn't use it with those plugs I'd been driving. All I had at the station was a worn old five-foot whip.

That was a bad moment there in the office doorway. And Uncle Ben Nunan came puffing up on the porch, poking at me a beautiful oiled black rawhide whip with a stock that had hand-worn silver decorations on it. "Been over to see Russ Thorp," he said. "Wished you luck. Thought maybe you'd like to be using this."

I guess that's when something began to happen inside of me. I stood there staring at an old man I hadn't been friendly to but who'd spoken for me at the right time, and holding the whip that belonged to a man I'd said small things about but who I knew was the best damn steadiest driver on the line and I wanted to cry. I wanted to burst out bawling like an overalled kid. And because I couldn't do that I let out a high-wide "Yippee!" and I stepped to the edge of the porch and put two fingers in my mouth and let out the high shrill whistle that was one of the Company customs and meant that a coach was ready to start rolling the whole length of the line.

We put on a good act. There was usually a crowd around to see a coach arrive or leave but they couldn't have told anything special was doing except maybe that I was strutting some and knowing I was new at it, they'd have been expecting that anyway. Bowen had loaded the safe himself in the coach up under the box when no one was around. Even the station tenders who had harnessed and hitched the horses didn't know the gold was there. When I whistled they brought the coach out, leading the horses and swinging with a flourish by the station porch.

That was the most beautiful sight I ever saw, horses and coach, and waiting for me to take charge. Six smooth bays, three matched teams; the leaders the smallest but still plenty big, quick-stepping and eager; the middle pair balanced for a steady pull; the wheelers the biggest, broad and weighted for any load; and power and speed and good deep bottom plain in every one of the six. And behind them a still new nine-passenger-inside Abbot-Downing Concord, the paint still bright, red body and yellow wheels, and shining brass side lamps.

I stayed on the porch leaning easy against one of the posts as I'd seen the other drivers do while Billy Skinner ambled out, shotgun casual in one hand, and climbed into the coach. For all you could tell he was just meandering along down to Stillwater where he lived. Race followed, taking his time, with the rifle crooked in one arm and the mail pouch hanging from the other. He tossed the rifle up on the box and strolled around to put the pouch in the boot and took his place by the coach door. The station agent came out with the two passengers we had, one a local storekeeper, the other some kind of a drummer with his carpetbag. Race checked their tickets and motioned them into the coach. He closed the door after them and reached and took hold of the handrail and swung himself in one quick motion up to the box. Then it was my turn.

I stepped down from the porch and walked around by the horses checking the harness while the two station tenders stood properly respectful holding the leaders. I fussed some with a couple of the bridles, unbuckling one and buckling it again in the same hole just to make it look like I was doing something. I went on around to see if the wheels were doped right. They were as I knew they would be, but that was always part of the act and a driver was supposed to make sure the greasing was thorough. That was his responsibility and if he let it slide and developed a hotbox out on the road he'd hear plenty about it from headquarters and every other driver he came across.

I had it timed right. I had swung to the box and gathered the reins in my left hand and was holding the whip in the other when Bowen appeared in the door of his office and held up his watch. "Ready?" he said. I nodded, trying to act like I'd been doing this for years. "Roll 'em!" he said and the tenders let go the bridles and jumped aside and I shook out Russ Thorp's whip in my hand and cracked the tip like a pistol snapping and those six horses settled like one into the traces and our wheels were rolling free.

We headed up the street at a nice pace and I swung around a couple of wagons and cut in close past the nose of an ox team to get in by the plank sidewalk as we went past Bentley's Harness Shop. For a moment I thought I would miss her, then I saw her inside the doorway and I let loose the highest, widest "Yippee!" I could drag out of me. I turned my head to look back and the sight of the surprise on her face as she jumped out of the doorway and shaded her eyes to peer after us was mighty pleasant. "Watch it," Race said and I turned my head forward again just in time to pull sharp left and avoid piling into a hay wagon someone was backing out of an alley. We straightened and the horses wanted to go and I eased them out a little to show things like that didn't shake me, and when we reached the turnoff I sliced around the corner without slowing much and steadied into the first long straightaway into the open country.

Race was riding the box the way he rode a horse, easy and relaxed. "Feeling spry, eh, Jess?"

"Damn right," I said. "These are real horses."

They were. They were letting me know it. They knew their business but they weren't sure yet did I know mine and they wanted to find out. They fiddled around some and broke rhythm a few times so I clamped down and showed them I could talk along the lines any language they liked, tough if they insisted on having that or friendly in a kind of partnership if they'd be the same. Inside of half a mile they were satisfied they could quit worrying about anything except an even pace and a square sharing of the pull. I could tell by the way they smoothed out, sending that little tingle of reassurance up the reins that makes a good driver's hands itch for leather when he's been away from it too long.

There never was and there never will be anything quite like it, the sweet singing satisfaction of driving willing horses and a well-built coach, the wind in your face and the hooves drumming and the wheels rolling rolling rolling into the receding horizon. At least that's the way it is when you're young, raw young, and life's still simple in sharp bright colors, with none of the graying gradations, and you're making your first main-line run with treasure tucked beneath your seat and you're driving beside a man like Race Crim.

I had the whole run pictured plain in my mind, every uphill climb and downgrade slope, and I treated my horses the way they deserved to be treated. The Company didn't skimp on its horses. They were bred right and trained right. They wanted to work. They'd have pulled their hearts out on the hills if I hadn't held them to a walk. I'd let them stretch into their reaching trot on the levels but never too much. And I'd help them on the down slopes, bracing my weight into the brake, holding back the heavy coach. They were still full of fight when we slid to a fine-style stop at Ten Mile station smack exact on schedule. Race picked up the mail and we shed the storekeeper and took on a cattle buyer and a Company blacksmith and were rolling on well within the regular four minutes.

Good as they were, those horses were tiring fast when we were nearing Lone Tree Ranch, our first swing station. They had to step along to keep Bowen's schedule. But they knew this was the end of the line for them so they perked and took us in with heads high and hooves slapping proud. They'd taken a ton and a half of coach and cargo twenty-one miles over uneven country in a shade under three hours.

The stock tender had the relay ready, big-shouldered brutes that must have had a lot of draft horse in them. They'd need it for the mountain stretch ahead. He had them in the traces and together we snapped the buckles and I'd checked the wheels and swung up again and we were rolling again right on the dot of seven minutes.

I was plenty busy with my driving now. We were climbing constantly and the road curled to get around the rock formations and there were places where sliding stones made the going rough. This wasn't the fun kind of driving where you step along and feel distance dropping away behind you and the wind of your movement always talking to you. This was hard work, uphill plugging, slow and dragging, and you had to pick spots where there was a bit of level and the coach wouldn't roll back, so you could stop and give the horses a breather. It was lonesome country and just about no other traffic was moving except once we met a three-wagon bull outfit and lost two minutes waiting for the whackers to swing their slow yokes to the side and clear the way.

"Dull like this, ain't it?" Race said. "Makes you want to lay the whip into the horses and see a little action."

"Damn right," I said. "It sure does." Then for some reason I wasn't irritated at the slow pace the horses had to give us. I was irritated at Race Crim. Not much but enough to make me think some. He had no call to be talking about my horses like that. I could tell what they were doing. I could feel it up through the reins, the hard slugging action of their heads as those big shoulders moved in rhythm and they kept that heavy coach moving steady and sure up a tough grade. They were working. He wasn't doing anything but just being pulled along.

Then I wasn't irritated any more. He was doing his job too. He was sitting there, easy and relaxed, and you might think he was lazy loafing. He wasn't. He was watching. His eyes were moving all the time and he was watching anything and everything around us, ahead and to the sides, and sometimes he'd swing his head to look behind. Not a thing moved anywhere in sight that he didn't see. Let a rabbit skip around a rock far ahead and he knew it. Let a breeze stir a small whirl of dust way off to one side and he was watching it and his mind was checking what it might be. He was riding messenger with treasure aboard and whatever might happen he would be there meeting it. Thinking of that I began to be a little nervous. If anything was going to happen, along here would be the place, where there was plenty of rock cover and we couldn't make a fast run.

I was nervous but nothing happened and we rolled over the hump and started down the other side. This was hard work too, a different kind. The heftiest man that ever lived couldn't hold a coach with the brake on some of the down stretches. With lighter horses we'd have had to fasten on a drag or chain the wheels. These horses could sit back, holding not pulling the coach, and let the whole weight be bearing on them and still keep it moving steady and even. *Bowen ain't so bad*, I thought. *He knows something about handling a stageline. He has the right stock right where it's needed.*

It was early and the air was chill but the horses were steaming when we stopped at Halfway. They were ready to quit and I couldn't blame them. It was only eleven miles up and over the hump but every one of them was hard going. There was no hurry with the relay this time because we had twenty minutes. Halfway was almost a small settlement and one of the eating places along the line. It had a few houses in addition to the Company building, and a man and his wife who lived in one served meals, good meals, all you could eat for a quarter per person. While the horses were being changed all of us went in, Race and Billy Skinner and I and our two passengers. The food was waiting, hot and tasty. "Jess," Billy Skinner said. "You're doing fine. On the inside it's been comfortable. No more jolting than the road's at fault for." —"Outside the same," Race said. "You're clocking it so careful Russ Thorp couldn't do better." With those two talking like that I had a busting appetite and did my share of cleaning off the table.

We went out and climbed aboard, all of us except the blacksmith. He was staying at Halfway because they had several days' work waiting for him there. That was his life, several days at one station then several at the next and so on, working his way up and down his section of the line and sometimes making a quick trip by wagon out on the road when there was an emergency breakdown call. When I shook out the whip and started the wheels rolling I found these horses were like the first ones, maybe not as gamy but about as willing to give what they had. The sun was dropping behind the big mountains far over on the right now and dusk was creeping through the foothill country we were in. A half-mile out we met the up-coach and stopped just long enough to swap greetings. "Watch the ford when you hit it," the other driver said. "Water's a mite high." And the friendly way he said that, like we were brothers in the driving business, was better than any drink I ever had in me. This was the life and no mistake about it. As we rolled on I was feeling I could drive as far as roads went anywhere out across the whole world.

It was clear dark when we stopped at Little Creek. The lights of the rancher's cabin were cheery as we drove up. It wasn't a regular stop, only when there was a call for it. We stopped this time to drop the cattle buyer. He'd told Race he was spending the night there to scout the country for stock in the morning. That left us with only the drummer as passenger which, except for the gold and the mail, couldn't be claimed a paying load. But there wasn't much down-traffic at our end of the line, not till you reached Stillwater and went on south toward the bigger settlements and the railroad. Traffic on our section was mostly up, north to Goshen, people heading there and moving on any way they could to the gold creeks. I figured to light the side lamps but Race took hold of my arm. "No sense advertising," he said and we started on, not more than three minutes behind schedule and we could make that up easy within a few miles.

We were rolling toward Big Creek, the next swing station. The moon was climbing out of the foothills ahead of us, first on one side then on the other as the road curved in big sweeps following the lower levels. I was a little tired, nice tired, with that poky run from the Gap in the morning and now this real one. That didn't make any difference in my driving because whenever reins were in my hands the driving part of me was awake. But maybe I acted sort of drowsy. Race leaned over and poked me in the ribs. "Been a long day, eh, Jess?"

"I'm all right," I said. "I'm fine."

"Not far to Big Creek," he said. "Then it's change horses and a straight run into Stillwater. Mostly nice downgrade."

"I know this road," I said. "Only one bad place left, cutting it through that short pass by Twin Rocks."

"Yes," he said. "Nothing much for you except coasting on in. We messengers now, we have it tough. I'll be riding this coach down the line rest of tonight and all day tomorrow. Wear out four drivers by then."

"Sure," I said. "And then you'll have three whole days to just loaf around. Meantime us drivers'll be moseying right along with our fifty-sixty miles each and every day. Least-ways I hope I will, if Bowen'll have sense enough to keep me on this run—damned if I don't make him."

"Don't blame you," he said. "Crowd your luck's the way. When a thing breaks, bull into it." He settled back some on the seat and maybe got a little drowsy too. There wasn't much need for close watching. This was open country spreading out clear on the sides, not giving much cover more than would hide a jack rabbit or two, and the moonlight let you see pretty plain. I settled back too and started thinking over the road we'd traveled, now that I'd driven it from a stage box. I was figuring how I might space the paces better to give the easiest riding and the fairest treatment for the horses if Bowen'd let me keep on and make the return run to Goshen the next day. I was thinking what I'd say to him over the wire from Stillwater and I was enjoying my own choice of words. And then the stand of trees along Big Creek was shaping in the moonlight ahead and we could begin to make out the dark bulk of the Company buildings, the cabin where the two stock tenders lived and the long reach of stable beside it.

"Easy," Race said, sitting up straight beside me. "Bring it in slow. Don't see a light anywheres about."

He was right. Not a light was showing, not in the cabin or the stable. The whole place was dark and quiet. There wasn't a sound anywhere in the whole world except the slowing beat of our horses' hooves and the soft roll of the wheels in the dust and the slight creakings of the coach body on its leather thoroughbraces.

We drifted to a stop in front of the buildings part way into the dark shadows of the trees. The ground sloped a bit backwards and I had to keep my foot on the brake. I could make out chock blocks ready on the ground.

"Billy," Race said, leaning over the side. "What do you make of it?"

Billy Skinner must have poked his head out the window. I could hear his voice float upward and over the top to me. "Smell's funny, Race. Too damn quiet."

"Maybe," Race said. "Maybe not. Could be those damn tenders found a bottle and are sleeping it off. Had that happen once." He hesitated a few seconds. "Hop down, Billy.

Chock the wheels and take a look around. Stay in sight and I'll cover you from here."

I heard the door on Race's side open and then Billy Skinner slapping the chocks against the wheels. I eased my foot off the brake and felt the coach settle against the blocks and I was pulling the leg under me so I could stand and look around when the first shots came crashing from along the stable wall. I heard a gasp from Billy Skinner and a strange sickening sound that could only have been him crumbling to the ground, then the battering volley was a sustained roaring in my ears. The front wall of the stable was a line of flame as the shots poured out and the bullets smashed through the coach. I was frozen in position, half up, half crouched on the box, and above the roar of shots echoing through the stable I could hear other sounds, a wrenching scream from inside the coach and the sharp open-air report of Billy Skinner's revolver from the ground behind us and the deeper coughing blast of Race's Spencer as he knelt beside me and fired as fast as he could pump cartridges into the firing chamber.

Time stopped and all sound with it and into the moonlit silence came Billy Skinner's voice, faint and his and yet not his as if it was somehow no longer a part of him. "I'm gone," it said. "Get the coach moving. Take it out of here." And while I was still hearing the words the shots began again, building their line of fire along the stable wall and the bullets searching for us.

"Like hell I will," Race Crim said. He towered on the box beside me and tossed the rifle at me. "I'll burn them out of there." He ripped open his jacket and leaped out from the box. He hit the ground with both revolvers blasting and he ran angling toward the stable to drop down behind the watering trough not more than twenty-five feet directly in front of it. The shots from the stable slowed, narrowing to the trough, and Race was snapping answers over it at the flashes.

I didn't know what to do. With the coach part way into the tree shadows I guess those in the stable couldn't make out whether anyone was left on it. I still held the reins in my left hand. The horses were too well trained to take off, but they were fidgeting and dancing and they didn't like this at all. There wasn't a sound from inside the coach or from where Billy Skinner was. I was sort of to the side of the

scene now, almost as if off in my own private world, watching
by the dimness of the moonlight and the spurts of powder
flame Race Crim shooting it out with he couldn't know how
many men inside the stable. I was there on my coach that
was mine as long as I was its driver and with treasure there
under me, and I didn't know what to do. And suddenly I
wasn't frozen or scared or wondering about anything. I was
mad through every inch of me. I wrapped the reins around
the brake and I grabbed the rifle and I started blazing with
the few shells left in the magazine.

That did it. That started bullets my way. I heard Race
shout: "Good boy, Jess. Pour it to them." But I didn't have
time to empty the magazine before what felt like a hot iron
slapped me along the right side and I stumbled backwards
off the box and thumped the ground flat on my back so hard
every bit of wind was knocked out of me.

I couldn't move. I could see and feel and hear. I could
see the sky clear with the mooncast over me. I could feel
the fire burning in my side. I could hear a voice in the stable
shouting something about the safe. But I couldn't move except for my ribs arching and aching for air. And while a
renewed burst of shots pinned Race behind the trough two
men who must have slipped out the rear door came around
the side and into the shadows by the coach and yanked the
safe down. I heard it bump on the ground and through the
wheels I saw the darker shadow of one of them lugging it
away and as I began at last to struggle over on my hands
and knees and try to rise I heard the other man shouting
and slapping at the horses. They couldn't take that. The
coach began to move. I was staggering on my feet by the
time the rear wheels were going past and I swayed toward
it and managed to grab hold of the boot going by. My feet
dragged till I got them working and I jumped with them
and heaved and pulled with the fire in my side spreading
fast and got myself up on the boot.

The horses were running ragged, seesawing in the harness. With the reins caught around the brake their heads
didn't have free play and they were fighting the bits and
jumping all over the road. The coach bumped and swayed
and I had all I could do trying to crawl over the top. It was
lucky the horses had enough sense to stay in the road if you
could call the crazy sidepitching they were doing staying in
the road. They splashed through the ford and the water was

high, almost to the coach floor I guess, and for a few seconds I thought the whole rig was going over. I hung on and crept crawling forward. I was nearly to the front when the coach sideswiped a tree and there was the sound of wood cracking. I thought sure a wheel was gone. But the coach kept rolling. I tumbled onto the box and clawed for the reins. I braced my left foot on the brake and began fighting for control of my coach. It must have been a third of a mile more before the horses were stopped, quivering and jumpy, but stopped. I talked to them a couple of minutes and when I thought they would stand, climbed down. There were bullet holes all along the coach. One of the wheels had several spokes broken but was holding. The right-hand door was still open and its hinges were sprung from the flapping it had been doing. I was afraid to look inside but made myself do it. There was a shapeless bulk jammed on the floor between seats that had been our passenger. I touched it and the feel alone told me no life was in it.

I stood by the door staring in and not even thinking, for I don't know how long. Moonlight through the window glinted on metal and I reached and it was Billy Skinner's shotgun. With that in my hands I felt better and I put it on the box and climbed up, and the pain streaking through my side made me remember all that had happened. Blood was in my shirt and soaked into the jacket, but the wound must have stopped bleeding because there was no trickling against my skin. I saw a good spot ahead and swung the horses around there and started back along the road and there was not a sound of any kind anywhere ahead of me. Once I thought I heard a horse whinny far off in the broken land to the left but I couldn't be sure. I stopped near the ford and left the coach there and with the shotgun ready in my hands waded across the creek and moved toward the station, hugging into the darkest shadows.

The buildings loomed ahead and I peered out from the trees. The dark still shape that had been Billy Skinner lay lost and lonely in the road. That was all. The space behind the watering trough was empty. The moonlight shone on cartridge shells in the dust there and I could hear the slow drip of water from holes in the trough. I could even make out the blurring in the dust where Race had crouched. But he was gone into the night and a strange kind of lonesome fear took me. I was the only living person in the whole lonely stricken land.

I jumped. I had heard steps inside the stable. While I watched a light appeared inside and moved along the windows. The very fact that someone else was alive and moving drove strength again into my muscles. I crept close by the cabin and along its front wall to the stable, intending to sneak a look in a window. Just as I neared the first one there was a shot inside, a single shot and no more. I leaped to get behind the rain barrel at the cabin corner where it butted out from the stable. I must have made some small noise because the light dimmed swiftly and disappeared and gradually I was aware that the small door beside the big closed barn doors of the stable was open and someone was standing in it. He was a dark shape, blacker against the darkness behind him. I strained my eyes and at last I could distinguish his outline and I realized that nowhere in the world could there be two men like that.

"Race," I whispered. "Is that you?"

He could not have heard what I said because at the first beginning of my voice he was moving and the roar of a gun drowned my words and a bullet whipped into the rain barrel in front of me.

"Race," I said fast as I could push out the words, "it's me. Don't shoot. It's me. Jess."

"You're lying," he said and his voice made me cold and shivering. "Jess's dead. Everybody's dead. You too. Come out where I can see you before I kill you."

"No," I said. "No, Race. It's me. Jess. I was on the coach. I've brought it back."

I was afraid to come out and he came and pulled me out and peered at me close and he seemed strange to me there, strange and terrible in the dim light of the dying moon. He turned and went back into the stable and I followed and he found the lantern and lit it again and hung it on a nail on the wall. He swung toward me and I could see him trying to shake himself into his old easy manner. I could see too why he seemed so strange. His hat was gone and a bullet had ploughed across the top of his head taking the hair and some of the scalp in a jagged furrow. Blood was clotting there and some had dribbled down one cheek and along his jaw. His clothes were messed and dirty and one sleeve of his jacket was ripped all the way up above the elbow and flapping when he moved the arm. He grinned at me and the grin, cracking the dried blood on his face, was a strange and terrible thing too, but his eyes were the strangest and most terrible, bright and hot and reflecting the lantern light in tiny leaping flames. But he grinned and he even managed to lean forward with a poke in the ribs for me. "Surprised to see me, eh, Jess? None of those bastards'll get me. I'll live to get them all."

"That shot," I said. "Just now."

"Look around," he said.

I looked around. The stable had a forlorn and beaten feeling. The stalls, the thirty or more of them, were empty. The floor along by the front wall was littered with cartridge shells. And close in by the wall the bodies of three men lay sprawled in the limp carelessness of death. "The rest got away," he said. "They had horses stashed out back."

"But that shot," I said. "Just a minute ago."

"One of these wasn't finished," he said. "He is now."

I had to think of something else quick. "The gold," I said. He pointed behind me and I looked and saw the safe smashed open and empty. But I'd said the wrong thing. His face was worse than before and his eyes, hot as they were, chilled me through. He jumped and grabbed me by both shoulders. "I could hear them smashing it in here," he said. "How did they get it off the coach? You were on it."

"Not then," I said. "Honest to God, Race, not then. They'd knocked me off. Got me in the side here. I just could grab hold again when the horses started running."

He pushed me away hard. He stepped to the wall and swung a fist into it. He stood staring at the blood beginning to show on the knuckles. "Broke my record," he said. "Took it right under my nose. Me. Race Crim." He swung that face at me again. "Why didn't you take the coach out of here before they got it?"

"And leave you?" I said.—"Why not?" he said. "You don't think those bastards, it don't make any difference how many'd ever get me?"—"You wouldn't leave Billy," I said —"No," he said. "I didn't. Should have. Billy'd have understood. It's part of the job."—"But you didn't," I said.— "No," he said again. "I didn't. So I busted my record."

I wasn't afraid of that face any more. Somehow I was sorry for him. I had to say something else. "Horses," I said.

"The place ought to be full of them."—"See for yourself,"
he said.—"And the tenders," I said. "This station has two,
hasn't it?"—"Yes," he said. "But they're gone. I looked in
the cabin. If they're around they're keeping mighty quiet."

We looked around. We found one of them in a back stall.
He was dead. There wasn't much left of his jaw where the
bullet had hit. We found the other in the feed room. He
wasn't dead. He was hogtied on the floor. There was a piece
of feedbag cloth stuffed in his mouth and another tied around
his head to hold it in. When we unpeeled him he was stiff
and sore and his tongue was swollen but he could talk enough
in a funny thick voice to tell us what had happened.

His name was Bert Foley. It all began, he told us, a short
while after the up-coach stopped and changed horses and
went on. That would be the coach we met out from Halfway.
Bert and the other tender were rubbing down the horses
when a man they never saw before walked in the doorway
and said he was passing by and wondered could he have a
drink of water. Sure, Bert told him that was one thing was
still free gratis and no one had found a way to charge for
yet. And when someone did, the other tender offered, he'd
quit taking his once-a-year bath. Bert thought it a bit peculiar that the man didn't even crack a trace of a smile at
their joshing, but he started dipping water out of the big
can anyway and the other tender was rubbing away again
when the man pulled a gun. The other tender made a fool
play then. He dashed for the door and he got through all
right and just as he broke outside someone out there cut
him down with a single shot. The whole bunch of them came
in, two of them lugging the body, and there was seven of
them. Bert could tell from their talk they'd just as soon cut
him down too. The only reason they didn't was that the man
who seemed to be boss was peeved already at that one shot
and didn't want any more that could stir up anybody who
might be within hearing distance. They tied Bert and gagged
him and chucked him in the feed room and fastened the door.
He could hardly wiggle the ropes were so tight but he could
hear them talking and moving around and figure from the
sounds what they were doing.

They let out all the horses and hazed them a good distance
into the badlands behind the station. That was so there
would be no fresh horses around for any posse coming after

them. They knocked mud out of some of the chinks in the logs along the front of the stable so they could poke their guns through without having them show as they would at the windows. They were planning to wait till we stopped the coach and got down to investigate, then blast us all out of action in a hurry. They'd have plenty of time afterwards to get the gold and split it and scatter for the getaway. With luck and nobody near to hear the shooting there might not even be an alarm until people began wondering why the coach failed to reach Stillwater. That'd be several hours. And at that anyone starting out to check would have the fifteen miles from Stillwater to the station to travel before finding what had happened.

The boss man was so cold-blooded and thorough with his instructions that Bert was scared there in the feed room. Scared about himself, I mean. He was thinking they might finish him before they left. He was thinking they might get to worrying he would wriggle loose or remembering he had a good look at one of them and a quick look or two at the others. That was why he began feeling better when he heard our shots answering from outside and kept hearing more when Race was behind the water trough. It was Race and that trough made them change their plan. When they couldn't get to him they made the dash for the gold and busted open the safe right away. When they still couldn't get to him and he was getting to them with that deadly snap shooting of his, they cut out the back and away, probably figuring, and nearly right, that he wouldn't have a horse to help him get word out quick anyway.

"Seven," Race said. "Four left." I didn't like the way he said that. I'd had enough killing to last me a long time. He was looking at Bert. "Know any of them?"

Bert didn't. He thought he'd seen a couple of them one time or another, passing along the road, but he didn't know who they were.

"I know one," I said. I hadn't known I knew until just that moment. I guess I knew him when I was lying flat on my back by the road and heard his voice shouting in the stable but the knowing hadn't soaked through me till now. "Bert," I said, "did one of them have a scraggly mustache hanging down, kind of hiding his mouth?"

"Sure thing," Bert said. "The boss one. I remember now they called him Slater."

"That's not the name he was using," I said. Race was staring at me now. "That man in the Hatt House this morning," I said.

Race stared at me and his face hardened more and he flushed brighter in the lantern light. I thought he was going to say something to me but he checked and swung to Bert. "Where's the nearest outfit? Where can I wrangle a saddle horse?"

"There's a couple in a little corral up the creek a piece," Bert said. "They didn't know about those."

"Find me a saddle," Race said. "And a rope."

"What are we going to do?" I said. "We've got a coach out there."

"I don't give a damn what you do," Race said. "There's four still living." He didn't pay any more attention to me or to Bert after Bert brought him the things. He took hold of the two stirrups with one hand and swung the saddle over his shoulder and took the rope coil in his other hand and started out the doorway. He went out of sight and his footsteps faded toward the creek.

I felt plain sick. I was tired and my side hurt and I didn't know whether I ought to follow Race or what I ought to do, and to top it Bert was staring at me as if I ought to tell *him* what to do. I had to get away from his staring so I went outside and over to the cabin and sat on the doorstep. The moon was gone and the night was almost solid dark, and I could scarce make out the deeper darkness of the trees by the creek. Just the same I could see everything clear and sharp like a big picture in my mind. I could see the coach on the other side of the ford with the mail and a dead man in it and Billy Skinner dead in the road dust and the empty cabin behind me and the long stable with Bert staring in it and the man he had lived with dead there with him and three others to keep him company and Race out in the night riding by the light of the little leaping flames in his own eyes on the trail of four men. I tried to think and my mind simply stood still and watched that picture and the only things moving in it were Race and four shadows somewhere ahead of him. And then my mind stirred and did something it had not done for a long time. I wished that Tom Davisson was there to tell me what to do. And then I was standing up and I was hearing Tom Davisson tell me what he'd told me once a whole lifetime ago: *When there's something that's got to be done and there's no one else to do it, do it.*

I looked around and Bert had come out and was standing near, staring and waiting. "All right," I said. "Get the lantern and come along." I led the way to the creek and across the ford and the coach was where I'd left it, the horses standing with heads down and the weariness holding them still. I climbed up on the box and drove them back across the ford and to the station while Bert walked alongside with the lantern. I climbed down and took the lantern from him and set it on the ground. "Get some grain for these horses," I said. "Give it to them right here. A couple of quarts each. You can use buckets." While he was doing that I made myself reach in the coach and straighten the body of the drummer the best I could on the floor. I went to the dark shape of Billy Skinner in the dust and it was lying in a grotesque sprawl and the right arm was stretched out toward the stable and the right hand was clenched around the butt of his revolver. I reached down and pried the fingers loose and looked at the gun. Every chamber was empty.

"Bert," I said. I had to make him see that too. For an instant there was nothing else that could ever be as important as making him see that too. "Look. He emptied it before he went." Bert looked but he didn't want really to see. He wanted only to keep busy doing something. I looked down at Billy Skinner what seemed a long time, I shook myself a little and dropped the revolver in my own jacket pocket and reached to pick him up. The pain ran burning in my side again but I didn't care. I wanted to do this by myself. I picked him up and put him in the coach on one of the seats and I wrenched at the door until its fastener would hold. I checked the damaged wheel and decided it might do for a while. I couldn't have put another one on anyway. "Bert," I said. "I'm going on in. You start cleaning things some or maybe you'd better rest a while. Soon as it's light you be out after those horses they ran off. The Company'll be needing them."

I took the lantern and went over by the rain barrel and found the shotgun that I'd dropped there. I hunted around till I found the whip where it had fallen when the horses ran away. I set the lantern down and climbed up on the box with my things. "Get those buckets out of the way," I said and when Bert moved them I swung the coach around and headed across the creek again and along the road to Still-water.

The darkness after moonset is a bad time any way you take it. I was taking it alone on my coach. The horses were tired. They had made their run from Halfway to Little Creek to Big Creek, their regular sixteen miles, and had that run-away spree too and they were tired. They were into another fifteen miles now and they seemed to know that and they weren't going to waste themselves on anything more than a walk. That was all right with me. I wasn't in any mood for more movement. I sat hunched on the seat and let them walk and that was all I wanted to do—sit quiet and let time go past till what had to be done now was done, and that was move the coach along till the next driver could take over—and I was doing it.

I was alone on my coach. And then I wasn't exactly alone. Billy Skinner's revolver was in my pocket and his shotgun on the seat beside me and Russ Thorp's whip was coiled there too. It wasn't just me there on the box. It was me and Billy Skinner too, and Russ Thorp and all the drivers and messengers taking all the stages through all the nights they were running. And it didn't seem fair or right that violence could leap so suddenly at us as it had, so suddenly and out of nowhere without a beginning except the bullet blast of flame and without an end except the abruptness of death for some of us. But that was wrong. There was a beginning. A few words spoken without thinking that a sal-low-faced man could hear and get their real meaning. But even that was wrong too. Behind that was whatever had made that man, the sallow-faced one, and those that followed him, into the kind of men who could be triggered by the real meaning of those few words into the deliberate bullet-blast of violence. And there was no end either. Some of us were dead and some of them. But Race Crim was out in the night and the sallow-faced man and his three shadows and other men would be riding out and even when the four were dead too or caught and tried and the law was done with them would that end it all? I was hunched on the seat and for a moment I could see myself plain, maybe for the first time in my life, a young one, a raw young one, with plenty to learn and not so happy to have to learn it and lonesome along a dark road and afraid not with any direct physical fear but afraid of the unforeseen and the unpredictable in the journey of the years ahead.

A breeze crept out of the down slopes I was entering and after a while I was moving through drifting wisps of fog. This changed to rain, a fine drizzle, and I fished under the seat and found a slicker and put it on. The cool dampness helped the horses. The grain was working in them too. They edged into a dogtrot and began to lengthen stride. I clucked to them and they made it a good traveling trot and I sat up straighter and felt better. *To hell with Bowen*, I thought. *He wonders can I handle a coach and take it through. Well, I'm doing it.*

Far ahead a horse whinnied. I jumped and listened and couldn't be sure I'd heard. I stopped the horses and listened and far off was the faint sound of hooves. Several horses but not in team rhythm. Saddle horses coming steady and fast. I clucked soft to my horses and drove off the road a piece and stopped them. I set the shotgun across my knees and waited.

They came on. They were going past when one of my horses whinnied. They swerved toward me and became black shapes in the darkness, three of them, closing in. "Stop," I said. "Keep away or I'll spray buckshot all around."

They slowed and fanned out some. I heard one say: "Hey, it's the coach." And another, "Race. That you?"

"No," I said. "It's me. Jess Harker."

"Been looking for you, boy," one of them said. "I'm Rafferty."

I knew him then, John Rafferty, deputy sheriff who handled things down Stillwater way for Tom Davisson. They rode close and I could make out the other two, Clyde Morrison, station agent at Stillwater, and Gene Gamble, owner of a freighting line with headquarters there. They threw questions at me and I answered fast as I could trying to tell the story straight. Soon as they had the gist of it Rafferty shut me off. "Take your coach in," he told me. "Hurry ahead and start using the wires," he told Morrison. "Swing around and wake the country to meet me at Big Creek," he told Gamble. "I'll take charge there till Tom can get along." He and Gamble whirled their horses and headed away in the rain. Morrison waited just long enough to say, "Be waiting for you, Jess," before he did the same.

I was alone on my coach again. I was peeved that they

hadn't said anything about me, about me hanging on to the coach and saving that at least for the Company. They hadn't even asked was I hurt bad. There wasn't anything else to do so I clucked to the horses and kept them moving slow till I found the road, then I made them step. I wanted to get that driving chore done. I don't know how far it was on to Stillwater but it was about the longest distance I ever drove. I was stiffening all over and chilled through, and the drizzle was working past the slicker coat down my neck. *Bowen can have his coach,* I thought. *Damned if I want it.*

When I rolled into the light from the Stillwater station windows things happened fast. Another coach was waiting with two men already on the box. Someone hurried to get the mail out of my coach and put it in the other. Passengers scrambled out of the station to climb in and grab seats and I could hear them grumbling about the delay. Someone started unhitching my horses and people were scurrying around to get that other coach on its way and nobody paid much attention to me. I didn't realize quite how stiff and sore I was till I tried to climb down. I made it by hanging to the handrail and easing down slow. I had a little trouble with the three steps to the station porch because my feet seemed to catch on them. I went into the waiting room and found a chair. After a while Morrison came in from outside talking to himself. "Four hours. Four hours late. Worst we ever had." He saw me. "Well, Jess. Was wondering where you were."

I pushed up from the chair and stumbled a step or two and caught myself. "God damn it," I said. "You and your whole goddamn stageline. I've got a bullet hole in me." I saw him starting toward me and the floor rocking and then rushing at me and that was all I saw for quite a spell.

It took me several minutes to figure where I was when I started seeing things again. I was lying on a cot in a plain room. My clothes were on a chair by the cot. There was a wide old wardrobe in the room and a table with a couple of notebooks on it and another chair. On the wall by the doorway was a row of hooks with some coats and a hat hanging on them. On the opposite wall by a window was a shelf with a few books and some shaving things. On the wall by the cot was a calendar with X marks knocking off the days. On the last wall opposite that was a colored picture of a white farmhouse with pink hollyhocks growing around it and un-

derneath the words: *Home, Sweet Home.* And under those
someone had printed with ink smears: *Not so sweet!* I looked
around, rolling my head on the scrubby little pillow, and
figured this must be the rear room of the Stillwater station
where Clyde Morrison stayed.

I could see sunlight outside the window, what looked like
late morning sunlight. I started to sit up and found I was
stiff as a weathered plank and naked as a jaybird under the
blanket. Not quite. Someone had bandaged my side and
taped it so I felt like I was wearing a piece of armor plate.
I squirmed and made it to sitting on the edge of the cot and
was trying to calculate how I could bend enough to get my
clothes on when I heard a little cough and swiveled my head
to see this plump little gent with a goatee in the doorway.
I grabbed at the blanket to pull it around me.

"A waste of energy, Mister Harker," he said. "I am already intimately acquainted with your person. Doctor Schlegel is the name. You've been honored with one of my best
bandaging jobs."

"Doc," I said. "You did it too good. I can't bend."

He chuckled and it I hadn't felt so bad, all hollow and
gone inside, I'd have been liking him plenty. "Maybe overdone a bit," he said. He came over and started peeling strips
of tape, talking all the time. "An excess of zeal, Mister
Harker. Too good an opportunity to miss. Not often a patient
so obliging, out cold and unable to fight back. Bandaging is
downright enjoyable. So neat and efficient. Not like messing
with a man's insides." He stepped back. "That better?"

I tried and found I could bend some. "Easy," he said.
"Don't pull those muscles. Now let's clothe the nakedness."
Damned if he didn't pick up my things, piece by piece, and
hold them for me to wiggle into. I fastened my belt and had
to sit down on the cot again. "Doc," I said. "What's wrong
with me?"

"Mister Harker," he said. "You have bruises up and down
your backside that could have been made by someone beating you with a board. A big board. You have a very nice
slice along your fourth rib. You have lost some blood and
probably are suffering some of the aftereffects of shock. You
also have the constitution of a young he-goat. There is not
a single solitary damn thing wrong with you that a good
meal won't cure."

He was right. I was feeling better by the minute. Better

and hungrier. "Doc," I said, "what do I owe you for the patchwork?"

"Don't try to cheat me," he said. "My bill will be submitted to the Company. That way my conscience will let me charge more."

I stood up and when the walls stopped waving I got into my jacket and started out with him pattering beside me. The station was deserted. The telegraph key was clattering like crazy but no one was around. "Doc," I said, "where is everybody?"

"Morrison is around town somewhere," he said. "But about the only one. Only man that is. They are all out riding the hills. Trying to be heroes. Must be the biggest manhunt in the history of these parts." We were out on the porch now. "Old as I am," he said, "and office-broke and lazy, I might be out too. But I have another patient. A much more interesting case than yours. The bandaging is more of a challenge. A nice hole through the shoulder. Very interesting. It even clipped a corner of the lung."

"Who is it?" I said.—"A man named Gamble," he said. "Gene Gamble."—"When was he shot?" I said.—"Early this morning. About sunup from the looks of the wound. They brought him in a few hours ago."—"Who shot him?" I said.—"Race Crim," he said. "Must have been an accident. Well, duty calls me back to his bedside."

I watched the plump little figure of this Doc Schlegel go trotting down the steps and angling across the street. He hadn't noticed or wouldn't notice how his words had hit me. And I wouldn't think about it. I wouldn't let my mind pick at it. By the sun I could tell it was around noon. I looked both ways, up and down the street, and there wasn't another man in sight. Matter of fact, the only living person in sight was a woman in the doorway of a place, right across, where a sign said *Eats*. I went across and she stepped aside to let me go in and followed me. I sat down at the low oilcloth counter and she went around behind it. "Lady," I said. "I want a double order of everything you've got."

"It's stew today," she said. "It's stew you'll get." She dipped a plateful and slid it in front of me, and a fork and spoon. She poured me a cup of coffee and slid it slopping toward me. She watched me eating. "Why'n't you out there too?" she said. "Scared?"

"Yes," I said. I didn't want to talk about what was happening. Not to her. "I'm scared green. That's what gives me an appetite."

She watched me a while. She took the plate and filled it again. "I know," she said. "You're the boy brought the stage in. They said he was a young one."

"Sure," I said. "Hitched myself up and pulled the damn thing myself."—"Why'd you let 'em get the gold?" she said.—"Gold?" I said. "What gold?"—"Don't be so smart," she said. "Everybody knows of it now. They got near a quarter-million in gold and you let 'em take it."—"Sure," I said. "We unpacked it for them and handed it over real polite."

She took the plate and filled it again. She reached for a pie tin with half a pie in it and started to cut a piece and stopped and shoved the tin by my plate. She watched me eat. I almost finished the stew and did fair enough on the pie.

"You and that Crim," she said. "What're you getting out of it? How much of the gold they giving you?"

"Shut up," I said. I got off the stool and looked at her across the counter. "What do I owe you?"—"Nothing," she said. "Not you." She was staring at me and her face was sort of fixed in that stare and it bothered me. "Thanks, lady," I said and started for the door.

"I don't want anything," she said. Her voice was tight and funny and I turned to look at her again. "My name's Skinner," she said.

I stood there feeling foolish and maybe looking the same. I reached in my jacket pocket and took out Billy Skinner's gun. I went over and laid it on the counter. "This was his," I said. I had to make her see how it was. "He died still holding it. Aimed at them. He fired every last bullet in it."

"What did that get him?" she said.

"I don't know," I said. *What the hell*, I thought. *What does doing things ever get anybody?* Then I did know. At least something. I knew what Tom Davisson would say. "He died doing his job," I said.

She picked up the gun and held it in her hands looking at it.

"Race wouldn't leave him," I said. "Race jumped down and went after them."

"I know," she said. "I was just talking. Billy and me

didn't get along real well, he was on the road so much. But he was mine all the same." She put the gun on the counter and pushed it with a finger. "You take it. It won't do me any good."

I took it and put it in my pocket again. There didn't seem to be anything more I wanted to say or could say so I left her and went out and across to the station. I saw Morrison coming from the stable and I went in and waited for him. He came in hurrying and nodded at me and dashed to the telegraph desk. He threw a switch that stopped the thing clattering and began pounding the key himself. He'd pound awhile then stop and let it chatter and then pound it again. After ten minutes or more he shut it off complete and swung toward me. "How's the side?" he said.

"Most of it still seems to be here," I said. "But what the hell's happening around Big Creek?"

"How would I know?" he said. "There's no key there. No one to operate it if there was. That was Bowen I was talking to. He wants a report from you. Crim hasn't checked in anywhere yet. The damn fool's skipped his job complete. You're the only one can give us the whole story."

I gave it to him best I could. I answered his questions and told him what had happened, filling in around what I'd told out on the road, and he jotted notes. I told him everything except one thing. I didn't tell him what happened in the Hatt House. I just said I knew who one of them was because I recognized his voice from hearing him talk around Goshen. Morrison took his notes and swung back to the key and opened it and started chattering with it again. I was fed up with waiting and the silly clicking when he quit. "All right, Jess," he said. "You feel able to do some driving?"

"Damn right," I said.

"Well," he said. "The line's pretty well straightened out now. Bowen has a driver coming in here for the up coach to Goshen this afternoon—"

"Like hell he has," I said. "I'm driving that coach. This is my run."

"It's your run," Morrison said, "when and if Bowen says it is. Just because you filled for Thorp yesterday doesn't mean a thing unless he says so. He ain't said so. You're pulling out of here in a few minutes. That's what he has said. Those horses you brought in last night belong up at

Big Creek. You're taking them there. With a wagon. You're waiting there and riding the coach when it comes on to Goshen so you can report to Bowen personal."

"A wagon?" I said. "You expect me to drive a wagon?"

"I expect you to do what you're told," he said. "Look, Jess. It's not my idea. It's what Bowen says. They're needing coffins at Big Creek and the horses belong there. You're to take them. Where'd I find another Company man right now to do it?"

"All right," I said. Here they were pushing the baby end of things at me again. "I'll go. But maybe I'll go just so as to get to Bowen to tell him what I think of this lousy outfit. Where's that lousy wagon?"

"In the stable," he said. "Loaded. I'll help you harness."

It wasn't much of a wagon. The four coffins filled it. We hitched two of the horses to it and put the other four fanning out on lead ropes behind. I took Russ Thorp's whip from the seat of the damaged coach that had been pushed back in the stable for repairs. I coiled the whip and tucked it under the wagon seat. I wouldn't use it with a rig like that. I guess I didn't act very happy about what I was doing.

"Don't take it so hard," Morrison said. "Look at me. Been up all night. Everybody's out playing cops and robbers. Had to do the stablework myself this morning. If no one shows soon I'll have to get the relay teams ready."

I looked at him and saw he could really use some sleep. He had his troubles too. Everybody had troubles. *He's doing his job*, I thought. *I can do mine. But I don't have to like it*. I drove out on the road and headed for Big Creek.

The going was slow for a while. The pull team was willing enough but the four horses behind kept milling around and bumping each other and holding back. After a time I figured to try something. I fussed with the tie ropes and paired those horses and got them strung out like two teams, one behind the other. Damned if they didn't step along nice then. That was the way they were used to going. There wasn't any sense letting one team do all the pulling so when I'd gone about a third of the way I switched teams in the harness and about two thirds of the way did that again. That spread the pull out even. It was upgrade work and I liked to be fair with my horses.

The night rain had softened the road and there were plenty of hoofmarks plain in the muddy places. But no one passed me going either way. Once a couple of riders showed far to the left topping a ridge. Maybe they waved but you couldn't be sure at the distance. A jack rabbit skipped ahead for a few hundred yards. That was the only company clear to Big Creek.

A dozen or more saddle horses were tied to the hitching rail running out from the far end of the stable, some of them mighty tired. I hollered and Bert Foley came out and took the reins when I tossed them. "How you feeling, Bert?" I said.

"Some better," he said. "But there's enough for me without any digging. Tell them the boxes are here."

"Who's them?" I said.

He waved at the stable and I climbed down and went in. About half the horses were back in their stalls. The bodies that had been by the front wall were gone somewhere and the floor had been swept. About as many men as saddle horses outside were standing and sitting around at one end of the long open space in front of the stalls by the feed room. I knew most of them by sight. Some were from Goshen and the others I'd seen at one time or another in this Stillwater territory. And leaning against a barrel and whittling slow on a stick was Tom Davisson. They all looked at me, and Tom with them, but none of them said anything. That was the way it always was when something serious was doing and Tom Davisson was there. People just naturally waited for him to take charge. And when he took charge things happened. He gave orders not just because he was sheriff, and most people did what he ordered because that made sense. He looked plenty serious now and the other men too. And tired. He nodded at me and told the others to get busy with the burying and he'd be out soon to help and when they'd gone, nodding and speaking to me as they went past, he beckoned me toward him.

"Well, Jess," he said. "What took you so long? Left Goshen last night, soon as I heard, but thought you'd beat me here. Bowen said he'd start you with some boxes first light."

"Damn it, Tom," I said, "I had to be patched some."

He straightened against his barrel and snapped the knife shut. "You hit, son? Bad?"

"I'm doing all right," I said. "But I've got a slice along my fourth rib."

"Nobody told me that," he said.

"Damn right," I said. "Nobody's paid any attention to me much since the shooting started. I'm getting kicked around again. Bringing that lousy wagon when I ought to have the up-stage today."

"Easy, son," he said. "There's a lot doing."—"It ain't fair," I said. "Bowen just won't—" "Easy," he said. "Bowen's a good man. Just not sure about you yet. He thinks you're young."—"What's that got to do with it?" I said. "I showed him. I saved his coach. I took it through."—"Ain't that what you were supposed to do?" he said.—"Well, yes," I said. "Yes. I guess so."—"Don't go throwing your chest out about it then," he said.

He looked at me and his face was hard as it had ever been but his eyes were still different. "You are young, Jess," he said. "But my money's on you the way it's been for a long time. You worry me some but there never was a maverick worth his salt didn't do that." He reached and pushed me a little on one shoulder like he did sometimes when I was a kid. "Don't worry me now, Jess. Too many things on my mind. Foley's talked and we know what you told Rafferty. The story's straight enough. Only one thing bothering. You were here. You tell me."

I waited and when the question came it was what I thought it might be but it still hit me like a blow low in the stomach. "What the hell's wrong with Race?"

"How do I know?" I said. "I haven't seen him since he started after them."

"None of us have," Tom Davisson said. "But we know what he's doing. He's combing the hills like a crazy man. Swiping a horse out of somebody's corral when he needs a fresh one. Shooting crazy at anything human that moves. He's scared hell out of a couple ranchers and plugged Gene Gamble bad. Rode up, saw he'd made a mistake, didn't do a thing. Just rode off swinging leather. That's not like Race."

"Maybe not," I said. "But if anybody gets those bastards Race'll do it."

"He's got one," Tom said. "Made it four. Some of the boys found the body. Race trailed him, though how in the dark licks me. They'd scattered, so that threw him off the others. But he got that one. No doubt about it. Drilled neat through the head. Some of the gold in a pouch sitting on his chest where Race put it to prove he was right. That's Race's way. Shooting wild at anyone shows ain't. Nor leaving Gamble lay."

Tom Davisson unsnapped his knife and started whittling again. "Race don't know it but five's the count now. Some of the boys fanning out from Stillwater got one. More of the gold on him. Chased him a piece and when he tried to shoot it they got him. We'll get the others. There's a string of men out from Goshen spread all the way from the mountains to the river, working down. Another bunch out of Stillwater, working up. By time they meet we'll have the last two. Could be before dark." He shaved a long sliver from the stick he was whittling. He pointed the knife at me sudden. "What's eating him?"

"Who?" I said.

"Race," he said. He looked me straight in the eyes. "Leaving the coach. Hightailing into the brush with a hot gun. Is it because he feels responsible?"

"I don't know what you mean," I said. I knew what he meant all right.

"Jess," he said, "it's my job to know more'n what happened. To figure why it happened so maybe it won't happen again. Here's how it tallies. One of those men, likely Slater, found out the gold was moving. You couldn't talk. You didn't know. I didn't talk. Thorp was home sick and couldn't. Billy Skinner didn't. Didn't know till just before you did. Bowen never left his office except to load the gold after he decided to move it. That leaves Race."

"There was Uncle Ben," I said.

"Too much sense," Tom Davisson said. "Race is my bet. His tongue's loose-hinged anyway. You hear him say anything?"

"No," I said. "Not a thing. What's eating him is easy. Those bastards busted his record."

Tom Davisson looked at me straight what seemed a long time. "That's it, Tom," I said. "It's got to be that."

Maybe my voice sounded queer. But his did too. "Won't push you, Jess," he said. "Maybe I don't want to know. We'll just call it that."

Not many afternoons stretch out long like that one. Tom and the other men had their burying to do but I wanted no part of it and stayed away. When they finished they split in bunches of twos and threes and wandered around waiting.

They'd wander near me sitting on the cabin step and start
asking questions and I answered the same damn questions
so many times you'd think I'd wear out the words. Then to
do something I helped Bert Foley get the relay teams ready
and when the up coach came along with four-five passengers
all excited to see the place and gabble about the robbery,
there were those same damn questions all over again. The
driver singled me out. "You Jess Harker?"

"Yes," I said. I didn't like him. I'd never seen him before
and he'd brought the coach in with a nice swing and he was
big and friendly but I didn't like him. He was driving my
run.

"Morrison says to pick you up here," he said.

"Morrison says wrong," I said.

"Better do as you're told," someone said. It was Tom
Davisson standing beside me. "Bowen'll be wanting to see
you."

"To hell with Bowen," I said. "I am staying here till it's
all over. It was my coach they jumped."

Tom Davisson looked at me and his eyes got as hard as
his face. "Do it your own way," he said and turned away.
And the coach pulled out with me still there and the waiting
began again.

The sun dropped further down the sky near the rim of
mountains to the west and things began happening again.
We heard the hooves first, a sound starting faint and growing till it was like an army moving, and then the riders
appeared in a big compact bunch coming down the road.
There must have been near fifty of them. John Rafferty was
in the lead, worn and tired like the rest. They came in by
the stable and swung down, all but one of them. This one
stayed in the saddle, hatless and slumped forward some,
and we saw his feet were tied with a rope under the horse's
belly.

Rafferty managed a grin at Tom Davisson. "Got another
one," he said. He went on telling how they got him but I
didn't listen. I was pushing close to the man still on the
horse so I could see him plain. It wasn't the sallow-faced
man, the one they'd called Slater.

Several men untied his feet and pulled him off the horse
and hustled him into the stable through the big main doors
that had been opened for the relay teams. They pushed him
into a corner by the feed room and he didn't try to stand,

just slid to the floor and sat with his legs out and his back to the corner. He'd look up at all of us crowded around and kind of glared at us, pulling his lips in over his teeth, then look at the floor like he didn't want even to know we were there. Tom Davisson stood facing him and looking down at him. "Foley," Tom said. "You recognize him?" Bert Foley edged close and studied the man. "That's him," Bert said. "That's the one asked for a drink."

"Slater?" Tom said.

"No," Bert Foley and I said together. Tom turned his head enough to look at me and I thought he might say something but he let it pass.

"No," Bert Foley said again. "But he's one of them."

"Sure he is," John Rafferty said. "We found this on him." He held out a leather pouch that wasn't much in size but you could tell it had heft to it. Tom took it and bounced it in his hands. "About eight pounds," he said. "We've got three of these now. All about the same." He stepped forward and kicked the man in the corner on the boot sole. "When you scattered which way did Slater go?"

The man didn't answer. He didn't even look up. Tom bounced the pouch in his hands again and started talking. His voice was soft, almost like he was talking to himself. "A nice smooth double-crossing kind of a rattlesnake, that Slater. It was a four-way split and there's maybe two thousand in this bag. There was twenty-seven thousand in the safe." The man looked up and surprise showed in his eyes, then his head was down again quick. Tom's voice went right on. "He's a smart man, that Slater. But only for himself. He plans for dirty killing even the meanest kind of decent road agent wouldn't touch and then he pays off cheap. Better'n twenty thousand's with him. Likely he's chuckling over it this minute." The stable was so quiet you could hear horses chomping hay in the stalls and Tom was talking steady in that soft voice and he had us all leaning forward a bit listening and the man was listening too. "Yes. He's smart, that Slater. He picks a good spot for the holdup. But it's a tough one for the getaway. It's tough enough the way the land lies but it's tougher because he's so smart he lets a kid get away with the coach and spread the word. Maybe there's one good way out. He takes that one himself. He leaves those who've been doing his dirty killing to scramble where they'll be caught. He's made murderers out of them and he gives them a thin slice of the big takings and leaves them scrambling where they'll be dead soon or facing a noose." And still in the same soft voice Tom added the words and aimed them at the man in the corner. "Which way did he go?"

Tom's voice stopped and in the silence the man's head came up and his lips pulled back in a snarl and he started to speak.

He didn't have a chance because another voice smashed the waiting stillness and battered at us with its taut bitterness. "Stop playing games with that bastard. Get out of the way and let me plug him."

Race Crim was in the big open doorway. How long he had been there no one of us knew. We had been intent on Tom and we were still caught now in the surprise of his speaking. He was grim and terrible in the doorway with the dried blood furrowing across his hatless head and the drawn tiredness written deep in his face and the little leaping flames in his eyes plain even in the late afternoon light.

The man in the corner froze, the snarl on his lips caught and held, all of him so still he seemed not to be breathing. Tom Davisson turned, slow and sighing. "There's been killing enough," he said. "It's not your private feud any longer, Race. This man's in the hands of the law." Race stared at Tom and Race seemed to shake himself with a little tremor that ran all through him and the flames in his eyes faded some and he reached up to wipe a hand across his face. He turned and went out and we could hear him working with the pump by the water trough.

Tom swung back to the man in the corner. "Which way did he go?" But the words were flat and useless now for the moment was gone and the man was looking at the floor again. Tom tossed the leather pouch he was holding to John Rafferty and reached and took the man by his clothes front and hauled him up quick and easy like it was a sack of grain he was handling and shoved him upright in the corner. Tom swung his hands, one after the other, palms flat and stinging, against the man's face, snapping his head from side to side. "Where was he heading?" The man didn't even grunt. He tried to spit at Tom and the saliva dripped on his lips. And Tom started swinging his hands again, steady and stinging, snapping the man's head. It was bitter and salt in your throat watching Tom Davisson like that. His face was hard, harder than I'd ever seen it, with the cheekbones like chunks of stone. He wasn't angry. There wasn't any emotion showing in him. He was a moving slab of iron doing what had to be done.

The man pushed out from the corner, striking blind, and Tom grabbed him by the shoulders and slammed him back and swung again. The man doubled down to hide his head with his arms and Tom struck him on the chin with a knee and drove his head up and swung again. The man stopped struggling and stood still, his head slumped forward and snapping with the blows, and suddenly he began to scream wordless sounds. Tom stepped back and the sounds died away and the man's chest heaved. "North," he said. "Slater went north."

"Back toward Goshen?" Tom said.

"Yes," the man said, hurrying the words. "That's right. Back that way. I saw him heading that way."

"Hell," someone said. "He's lying. No one could've got through us coming down."

"He was going to hole up," the man said.

"Where?" I guess half a dozen men said that.

"I don't know," the man said. "Honest to God I don't."

"Get him, Tom," someone said. "He's still alying."

The man looked at Tom like a dog that's been beat. Tom's face didn't change. "No. It figures. That'd be about the only way." The man let his breath out in a sigh you could hear all through the stable and turned into the corner and put his arms against the walls and sobs shook him clear down through his legs.

"Easy," Tom said. "It's over." He motioned to one of the other men to slide a box to him and put it against the wall and took the man by the shoulders and sat him on the box. He pulled a handkerchief out of a pocket and handed it to the man to wipe the sweat and blood flecks from his face. He looked around at the rest of us. "Anybody got a bottle?"

"Christ amighty!" Race Crim was in the doorway again, towering tall and eyes flaming. "Baby the bastard! What're you waiting for? You've got what you wanted out of him. Now let's swing him."

I could feel it running through the other men, the little tingle of excitement starting small and growing. They were tired and hungry and mad without really knowing at what had put them to riding all night and most of the day. They were torn inside some by what had been happening there

in the corner and tension had been building long hours in
them and they wanted to release it in a way that would be
big enough. Race could feel that too and he stretched taller
and his voice flicked at them. "We've got him dead to rights.
He's even admitted it. Maybe he's the one got Billy. Shot
him without giving him a chance. Why in hell should we
give him any?"

Race had them. Most of them. I could feel it in me, the
urge to act and by doing drive some of the high-stretching
bitterness out of me. They were shouting in a jumble of
voices and there was no doubt he had them. "Clear the way,
boys," he said. "I'll put a rope on him." They spread to make
a lane for him and he started forward.

"No!" Tom Davisson stepped out to stand in front of the
man shrinking down on the box. Race Crim stopped and
they stood facing each other. "Don't be so damn finicky,
Tom," Race said. "You heard the others here. You're out-
voted, Tom. It's out of your hands."

"No," Tom Davisson said. "This man is in the hands of
the law and I am the law."

"Tom," Race Crim said and his voice was flat and another
man's voice, "you and your law are too damn soft and slow.
Get out of my way." And the fingers of his hands hanging
limp at his sides began to curl and the hands drew up slow
till they were close to the grips of the two guns at his hips.

"No." Tom Davisson's voice was flat too and the voice of
another man and his right arm curved slightly by the gun
at his hip and he seemed to crouch as he still stood straight
there, broad and solid and a slab of iron. And all the rest of
us stayed as we were, motionless, caught as we had been
the instant he spoke. And the silence in the stable clamped
us immovable to the endless trembling edge of time. Then
Tom Davisson's hands came up slow, past the gun and on
up, and he crossed his arms on his chest. "Race," he said
and his voice was his own, "I expect I'm the one man in this
whole territory that maybe just might be almost as good as
you with a gun. But I'm not going to draw on you. There's
too many a good trail we've rode together. And you're not
going to draw on me. For the same reason. And for a better
reason. Because you know I'm right."

Race rocked slow on his feet. He shook his head, shook
it quick and hard and the shaking went down through him
and the fingers of his two hands uncurled limp. He put one

hand out toward Tom and made a funny small gesture like he was trying to brush away something in the air between them. He looked around at the rest of us and there were no little flames in his eyes. He was Race Crim the way we had always known him only he was weary with a weariness that showed in every part of him. He turned and started out the big doorway and we could move again and there were mutterings among us, angry and disappointed, and he stopped and turned back. "Tom and I could take the whole bunch of you," he said. The mutterings died away and he disappeared through the doorway and Tom Davisson caught the whole stable in his grasp by chuckling, grim but a chuckle, and speaking as if nothing much had been happening.

"You boys want to do too much of a good job. You've already done more than I've a call to expect. All but Slater's accounted for. It'll be up to me and Rafferty now . . ." He was telling them it was time to think about meals and getting home, but I wasn't interested. I edged toward the doorway and outside.

Race was easing the girth on the horse he'd been riding. He finished and leaned his elbows on the saddle and stayed there with his head down. I guess he looked tired and beat. But he could never really look that way to me. Not now. Not ever.

"Race," I said.

He swung around to lean his shoulders against the saddle. "Let me alone, kid. Get back in there with Tom. You can't go wrong with Tom."

"Race," I said, "the court'll hang him anyway. Do you really think Tom's right?"

"Tom says he's right," Race said, "so likely he is. Goddamn him, he's always right. You'd think sometimes a man'd get tired of being right."

"You did more'n anyone else," I said. "You did more'n anybody else ever could. You got four of them yourself."

He straightened from the saddle. He even poked me in the ribs. "You appreciate me, eh, Jess?" It was what he always did. It was what he always said. But it wasn't the same. There was that faraway look in his eyes like he was staring through me and past me into some dim distance beyond us. And then men were coming out of the stable and spreading to their horses and throwing awkward but friendly remarks to us and each other and riding off.

Tom Davisson and John Rafferty came out with their prisoner between them and tied him again on his horse. "You go back to Stillwater and watch things from there," Tom told Rafferty. "Slater'll be holed in good by now. Not much chance of smoking him out. But he'll have to make a move sometime and we'll be onto him. He's got that gold to slow him down." Rafferty mounted and rode off and Tom turned to me. "We're heading for Goshen, son. Better come along."

"Hell," I said. "I haven't got a horse."

"Never think ahead, do you, Jess," he said. "Foley's got one inside he claims will take a saddle. You're still with the Company till Bowen fires you which can't be till you get back. Take it."

When I had a saddle on the horse and led it out the others were starting up the road, Tom and the prisoner and Race and several of the men from Goshen who'd waited for them. I had a little trouble with the horse because it was a coach not a saddle horse and I was a driver not a rider but after some jumping around the two of us decided we could get along together. I caught up with them and we rode through the dusk into the dark, quiet with nobody saying much, past Little Creek without stopping, and on to Halfway. We ate there and bedded in the stable on thick straw. Tom put his prisoner in the feed room and tied the latch down. There wasn't any chance of the man getting away. He couldn't have got out without a crowbar and if he'd had one he'd have taken a while and made plenty of racket.

It must have been my rest in Morrison's room at Stillwater. My side bothered me too, not much because it was doing all right, but some. I couldn't get to sleep. I kept thinking over what had happened, step by step, minute by minute. The late moon was up and by its dim light through a window I could see Race on the straw a few feet away. He wasn't asleep either. He was staring at the dark beamed ceiling. I raised on one elbow. "Race," I whispered. He rolled his head and his face was lost in shadow but it was turned toward me. "Race. They didn't bust your record. Not really. You smashed them. You upset their plan. We'd all be dead and they'd be away safe if it wasn't for you. Some of the gold's back already. Slater'll be caught when he sneaks out of hiding and the rest of the gold with him and it'll be over."

"No." His voice came from the shadow, soft and barely reaching me. "It'll never be over. It's all or nothing in things like that. They got the gold. Getting it back can't change that." His head rolled back and I could see his face again in the moonlight, his eyes staring at the ceiling. I watched him and he lay there motionless and my mind picked at the terrible unbreakable problem of the violence without beginning and without end rushing out of the night at us on the coach and then I was there on my coach, standing up and working the lever of a Spencer repeater, and his voice was coming to me from the darkness behind the water trough where death sliced through the air all around him: "Good boy, Jess. Pour it to them."

That was wrong. He was laying on the straw and speaking to himself or to whatever he saw in the ceiling above him. "When they're all dead maybe it'll be better."

I watched him and his eyes closed and he might have been asleep. After a while I felt my arm getting numb and I lay flat. After a longer while I was asleep too.

The first sunlight striking through a window brought me awake. I lay quiet, just moving my head. Tom and the others were still asleep. Where Race had been was only the impress of his figure in the straw. I heard a small shuffling of leather and saw him, by the small outside door, buckling his gunbelts in place. He was doing this slow and careful, trying not to make any sound. While I watched he went over by the feed room, putting his feet down easy and keeping his weight on his toes. He stood there, staring at the feed room door, and my chest began to hurt and when he turned away I realized I had been holding my breath. He went back and took his jacket off a hook and fished in a pocket and found a pencil and an old envelope. He held the envelope against the wall and wrote on it and stuck a corner of it in a crack in the wall by the door. Still walking soft and easy he crossed the open stretch of the stable and disappeared among the stalls.

I raised my head and looked around. The others were still asleep. Not all of them. Not Tom Davisson. His eyes were open and he was looking at me. He raised a hand and motioned me to put my head down. In a minute or two Race came out from the stalls leading his horse ready saddled, wincing a little at the small dull sounds of its hooves on the straw. Quietly he opened one of the big doors and led the horse out and closed the door.

I sat up. Tom did too. We heard the hooves outside, faint

and fading. Tom rose and padded in his stocking feet over by the little door. He pulled the envelope from the crack and held it out at arm's length the way he always did to read things. The hand holding the envelope dropped to his side and he opened the door and stood in the doorway looking out. I stood up and went toward him and he heard me and stepped outside and I followed into the bright chill freshness of the morning. I reached and took the envelope and he let me take it. *Tom—I don't want to do that to you—if I stick around I'll plug him sure.*

"Do what to you?" I said.

Tom looked at me and his eyes were different in his hard face but not for me or the morning. He didn't really see me. "I've got a record too," he said. "Never lost a man for the court once I had him."

I thought that over and saw how it fitted. "What would you have done," I said, "if he'd opened the feed room door?"

"I'd of stopped him," Tom said.

"But what if you had to shoot to do it?" I said.

He looked at me and he saw me. "It wouldn't come to that. Not with Race." He took the envelope from me and folded it and tucked it in his shirt pocket. Suddenly he grabbed me by my shirt front. "But I'd do it. I'd shoot." He let go of me and padded away a few feet and swung back. "That's got nothing to do with keeping a record or anything like that. It's got to do with doing my job and what a man believes in."

"You'd shoot a man like Race," I said, "just to save a lousy bastard that's due for a hanging anyway?"

"Him?" Tom said. "He ain't worth a lead penny. Save him? In a way. Save him for a hanging. Sure, he'll likely swing. But it's who swings him and how that's important."

"Damned if I see that," I said. "Not important enough to shoot a man like Race."

"Listen, son," Tom said. "You believe a thing or you don't. You start making exceptions and you head into trouble. This is rough country out here. Rough and new. We're trying to get some law established because that's the only way most people can get along together and be reasonable decent and go about their business not worrying about their necks all the time. I say I'm the law but I'm only part of it. Somebody steps out of the line and it's my job to get him and turn him over to the court to decide is he guilty and what should happen to him."

"This one's guilty," I said.

"Sure," Tom said. "Guilty as hell. But it's not my job to say that or what to do with him. It's my job to give all evidence I can to the court and let it decide."

"When your law hangs him," I said, "he won't be any deader than if he was swung yesterday."

"But the whole job'll have been done right," Tom said. "Let Race and some of the boys hang him, maybe it'd be right this time. But they might get the habit. Next time maybe it'd be a man wasn't so sure certain guilty. Maybe one time it'd be a man wasn't guilty at all but it just looked that way." Tom stood on one foot and lifted the other so he could reach and rub it with his hands. "Blowing like this before breakfast," he said, "is bad for the digestion. Can't talk things like that into a man's head. If he has the stuff he feels it inside like Race did when I called him. Anyways I need my boots. My feet are cold." He padded into the stable and I followed and we waked the others and started getting ready for the ride to Goshen.

There wasn't much noise when we reached town. Not like I expected. But then the story was a day and a night old and had already been chewed over pretty much. Everybody knew, even about the man Tom was bringing in, because some of those who had been at Big Creek with the posse had ridden all the way home the night before. People wanted to have a look at him and that was all right. But they didn't crowd around asking questions like I expected. When we stopped by the building where Tom had his office in the front room with the jail behind, he asked me what I was planning to do.

"I was thinking of trying it up in Idaho," I said, "before all this started. Doesn't seem to me anything's happened to change my mind. Not the way Bowen's behaving."

The look in his eyes made me afraid he'd start giving me advice again. He didn't. "Think that over careful," he said. "You'll be having time for thinking. You can't leave here till after the trial. You're a material witness."

I didn't argue. I knew argument wouldn't change Tom Davisson. "When'll that be?" I said.

"The judge'll be through here on circuit next week," he said. "Probably then. Slater too at the same time if we have him."

I rode on around the block and down the street to the station and turned the horse I was riding in at the stable. I went up the steps toward Bowen's office slow because I was thinking what to say. I was thinking I'd hit him before he could me, by wanting to know why he yanked me off Russ Thorp's run and set me to hauling coffins. But when I saw him behind his desk with a pencil clamped in his teeth and the worry lines in his face I didn't say a word. I sat down on a chair and waited for him to speak first.

He took the pencil out of his mouth and started rolling it with his fingers on the desk. "Hello, Jess," he said. "So you decided to come in."—"Yes," I said.—"Had quite a time of it, didn't you?"—"Yes," I said.

He picked up the pencil and pointed it at me. "Jess. You still working for the Company?"—"I don't know," I said.— "Neither do I," he said. "Why didn't you ride the coach in here yesterday like Morrison told you?"—"I was in that holdup," I said. "I was going to see what happened."— "Thought Davisson and Rafferty needed your help, did you?" he said. "My God, boy, you are young."—"I don't feel so young," I said.—"Maybe not," he said. "You did a fair job with the coach. Can't say as to the driving because there's no one to report on that. But you took the coach through. That ought to square holding out yesterday. You can start driving again tomorrow."—"Where?" I said.—"Why, over to the Gap," he said.

There was a time, not more than two days before, when I'd have stood up and laid into him with plenty of words about a deal like that. But now I didn't. I just sat quiet. "No," I said.

He started balancing the pencil on one finger and I guess he was balancing more than a pencil. "That's too bad," he said. "Uncle Ben'll be sorry to hear that. It's kind of tough on him making that run alone."

"Uncle Ben?" I said. "Is he driving that old coach? He's no driver."

"The hell he ain't," Bowen said. "He was driving a stage before you were born. Got an arrow in his shoulder once and the arm's bothered him ever since. But he can drive when he has to." Bowen looked straight at me. "When there's no one else to do it."

That was new to me. Uncle Ben never talked about himself. I thought he'd probably been a lot of things with the Company at various times, filling in maybe at lots of things. But not a driver. I remembered how I'd talked in front of him. I remembered how I'd acted sometimes, showing off with the ribbons and using a whip when there was no call for it. I studied on this and Bowen waited. I stood up. "Mister Bowen," I said, "tell you what I'll do. I have to stick around here till the trial. I'll drive that old coach for you till then."

"That's damn nice of you," he said. He was being sarcastic but I didn't let that rile me. "You start looking for someone else," I said. "You get a good one for Uncle Ben."

"Still telling me how to run my business," he said. He wasn't being sarcastic. I didn't know what he was being and I didn't care. I went out on the porch and leaned against a post. *That's done*, I thought. Bowen had been told I'd be leaving and in about a week there'd be no more reason for my staying around and I could go off where people would take me as I was and not keep on treating me like a kid just because that was the way they had known me so long. I'd make a name for myself and some day I'd come back and men like Race Crim and Tom Davisson, yes and Bowen and Uncle Ben, would recognize me as men like them and I'd be one of them.

I shifted my weight from one foot to the other quite a few times before I realized what was wrong with me. I was damned lonesome and didn't have anything to do. Usually when I hit Goshen coming over from the Gap with the afternoon and evening ahead of me before a good sleep and the start back the next morning, I'd knock around town a bit and have a drink or two and talk with anyone about and wind up being with Mary Ella and eating supper with her and her father. Now I didn't feel like any knocking around and I didn't feel up to seeing Mary Ella, not after the way I'd tried that fool stunt of rushing her with marrying talk.

There was one thing I could do. I went to the stable again and got Russ Thorp's whip from where I'd put it when I checked in the horse and went up the alley behind the stable till I came to the small two-three-room house where

Russ Thorp lived. I knocked on the door and a pleasant-faced woman opened it and I realized with some surprise that in all the time I'd known Russ Thorp I'd never been to his house before or met his wife. Seeing her looking homey and just plain nice and worried, yet making out to smile at me, I had a feeling I'd been missing something, some one of the real things maybe people could get out of life. She seemed to know me right away. "Come in, Jess," she said. "Maybe it'll do him good to see you."

I went in and he was lying on a big old four-poster in the second room, flat on his back with his head propped on a doubled-over pillow. He wasn't a tall man but he was wide and thick and he looked strange with his wide shoulders and thick neck showing above the covers with a flannel night-gown around them. The flesh of his face was shrunk so that the outline of the bones showed and I could tell he had spent long hours fighting pain and maybe other things too. But his eyes brightened when he saw me. "Nice of you, Jess," he said. "Mighty thoughtful." His voice was weak but steady. "I'm kind of out of it. But you're not. Hear you took the coach through with a busted wheel and a bullet hole in you. Heard plenty about it."

"Who told you?" I said.—"Why, Bowen did," he said. "Who the hell else?"—"Well, I'll be damned," I said. But he didn't hear that. He was looking at the whip in my hand and he was starting to talk again and his voice was shaking. "Take it away," he said. "Keep it or throw it away. Smash it. Burn it up. Take it out of this house."

His wife was in the room with us and more worried than before and her eyes were pleading with me. "What's wrong, Russ?" I said.—"They've carved me plenty," he said. "They say I'll not drive any more. Maybe clerking or some lousy paperwork. But no driving."

I stared at him and I threw my mind around frantic and I saw a cap hanging on a hook. A small cap. "Russ," I said, "you've got kids?"—"Two," he said. "Girl and a boy. That makes it worse."—"No," I said. "That boy. He's damn lucky. He's got you to teach him to use this." I dropped the whip on the bed and I got out of there fast and as I pulled the door shut behind me I had a glimpse through the inner doorway of his wife sitting on the bed and one of his big hands holding one of hers.

* * *

I stood on Russ Thorp's doorstep. *A week*, I thought, *can be a damned long time*. I stepped down and walked a short ways. *There's only one person*, I thought, *I really want to see right now*. I went back along the alley to the street and up the street and turned into Bentley's Harness Shop, and the two of them were there where they always were.

Calvin Bentley raised his head from his stitching. "All hail," he said. "The hero cometh." He must have seen something about me that changed him because he put his arms behind him and leaned back on his bench. "Sorry, Jess. My tongue wags unheeding. That was from the lips, not the heart. We are glad to see you safe if not altogether sound. Don't mind my pleasantries."

"That's all right, Mister Bentley," I said. "My tongue can't keep up with yours so I don't even try."

"Very sensible," he said. "I am only the father, not the daughter. Save your verbal ammunition for her. She is a most unmanageable young lady. Was all for borrowing a horse when—"

"Be quiet, Father," Mary Ella said. She had set aside her book and was perched on the counter watching me. "Is it bad, Jess? Where you were hit."

"I'm getting around," I said. "Hell, I couldn't even get me a decent bullet hole. The doc at Stillwater almost laughed at me."

"It's nothing to laugh at," she said. "A slice along the fourth rib."

"How'd you know that?" I said.

Calvin Bentley chuckled. "Bowen told her. She pestered him till he had a full report and—Oh, all right, my dear. I will stick to my last." He took his needle again and started stitching.

"Maybe Bowen talks about it," I said. "But not to me. He wants to put me on that silly Gap run again."

"Are you going to do it?" Mary Ella slid off the counter and watched me like she was waiting for something important.—"Yes," I said.—"Why, Jess. That's wonderful."—"Like hell it is," I said. Like hell it was. She knew how I felt about that run and here she was siding with the others and still thinking about me as just a kid. "Wanting to put me on that lousy run again after what I did. I'm only doing it for Uncle Ben."

"Oh," she said. She seemed to be disappointed. "But you're going to stay?"

"Till next week," I said. "Till the trial." Then, because I was started talking, I kept on with what I'd come to say and I didn't care whether her father was there or not. "Mary Ella," I said, "just because I'm leaving next week and because you won't marry me, is that any reason we can't go on seeing each other the way we did till I do leave?"

She studied me awhile before she spoke like she had been searching for the words she wanted. "I'll always be glad to see you, Jess."

"What I mean," I said, "is can't we just pretend I never said anything about marrying and let everything be just the same as it was?"

"Yes," she said. "Yes, I suppose so."

But it wasn't. It wasn't the same at all. We did what we always did. I worked on a saddletree for her father while he went on with his endless stitching and she sat cross-legged on the counter watching us and all of us talking about anything that came to mind. She went back to the kitchen to prepare supper and I helped her father lay out and cut leather while he told me about books I ought to read and I thought there was no need for me to do that because he told about them so well and the two of us could hear her rattling pans and dishes through the intervening room. After we ate I washed the dishes and she dried and we left her father with his pipe and a book and the evening lamp lit and we walked, not along the main street, but along the back alley to the side street that led in just a hop-skip-and-jump to the open country where we could wander out and around and return, hand in hand, maybe arm in arm, not talking much, without being bothered by anyone. But it wasn't the same.

There was a barrier between us now, a constraint that kept us self-conscious even when there was no one, not even her father, to see us. Something was gone, a free and easy comradeship we had known, and nothing new had taken its place and it left an emptiness that was like a loneliness even when I was with her.

And her father didn't josh me any more, didn't wind me up in words the way he used to. Maybe it had shaken him some, realizing I wanted to marry Mary Ella, and he was worrying about that. Maybe he was worrying some about me, not as a possible son-in-law, but just as me, another human being bumping against the hard facts of living in an indifferent universe. Quite a few people were worrying about me then and I didn't even know.

It wasn't the same either when I'd leave Mary Ella and wander down the street to the Hatt House for an hour or two or maybe three with anyone who might be there around the bar or at one of the tables before going upstairs to the room I rented from Frank Hatt. I couldn't be easy with them any more or they couldn't with me and that amounted to the same thing. There was always one or two who had been at Big Creek when Tom's prisoner was brought in and they didn't know whether I had been with them when they wanted to follow Race and put a rope on him. They didn't know whether I stood with Tom or Race then. Either way would have been all right because it would have been definite and they would have known how to take me. But they didn't know which way. They couldn't. I didn't know myself. Sometimes I'd think one way and sometimes the other and the more I thought the more confused I was because I could go chasing back and back with reasons on both sides and like with the robbery itself there would never be a beginning or an end to the right and the wrong of it.

Nothing was the same. Tom Davisson was curt and quick with me. He'd let me hang around his office awhile when I came in from the Gap and went straight there to find was there any news about Slater. But he paid little attention to me and acted most of the time like I wasn't there. He didn't give me advice every time I turned around any more. He didn't give me any at all and it wasn't till now he had stopped I realized how much I had come to depend on it. Not always to take it, I mean, but just to have it slapping at me pretty regular, a part of the inevitable things of life like the weather and meals and the feel of reins in my hands. And Race Crim was a different person to me. Not just to me. To everyone. He hadn't gone back to the Company. He hadn't gone near Bowen's office. He slipped into town every day or two to ask if anyone had heard anything about Slater and slipped out again, leaner and harder and more deadly dangerous-looking each time, still hatless and wearing the same old Company jacket with the sleeve torn and the furrow across his head a jagged scab that would leave a bad scar. I saw him once and he let me buy him a drink, but nothing of the old easy familiarity was there and when I worried about the shrinking of his eyes into their sockets and told him he ought to get some sleep he startled me with the intense way he spoke. "I can't sleep," he said. "Not till they're all dead." And when I swung to the bar and turned back with another drink I thought might soften him, he was gone and was swinging into the saddle out front.

Nothing was the same. Except maybe Bowen. As far as I could tell nothing ever changed Luke Bowen. Not toward me. He was short and straightforward and just exactly the boss of his section of the line when he hired me and he never had been anything else and he wasn't anything else now. I was someone who worked for him and he told me what he wanted me to do and it didn't mean a damn to him whether I liked that and when I did anything he thought was wrong he told me off short and straightforward and that was that. If he hadn't been so obstinate about that silly Gap run I could have held my head up working for him.

But there was one thing that was better. The Gap run wasn't quite so bad because of Uncle Ben. He would talk to me now. I guess maybe he always would have only I hadn't encouraged him. To me he had been another of the old relics I had to work with when I thought I should have been uncurling my whip along the main line. It was peculiar how different he looked as soon as I knew something about him. He was really quite spry for a man so old he probably had lost count. What made him seem slow and fumbling was the way he moved and did things favoring his left arm, a mighty important arm for a driver. There was a lot written in his face when you took time to study it some, not just age and the kind of drooping of the flesh age brings. He had the same feel that came from Race when Race had been on the box beside me and we were slugging up and over the hump, the feel of being there and if anything happened being ready to meet it. Maybe he wouldn't have been able to do much after what the years had done to him, but he would be there doing his best.

I was a bit worried about talking to him when we started our crawl over to the Gap the next morning. I wasn't worried about him watching my driving. A good driver never worries about another watching because he knows a kinship's there that has nothing to do with personal likings and dislikings and the other one will understand what he's doing and make allowances for the unexpected things that can happen with horses. I was worried about the opinion he might have of me after the way I had treated him and the way I had laid my whip to those old horses when we went into Goshen the day the whole business started. He sat quiet and let me be first to speak.

"That was a fool stunt," I said, "whipping these horses the other day."

"It was," he said. Then a dry old chuckle came out of him. "Remember doing stunts like that when I was about your age." We jogged along. "Time came I steadied down," he said. And after that we got along fine and when I'd poke and pull at him with questions he'd tell me some about the early days when the western stagelines were starting and the first coaches weren't coaches at all but wagons rigged with seats and maybe in bad weather a chunk of canvas pulled over some poles—and the winters were really bad. "Don't seem to be so bad now," he said. "Remember a time near froze, even with a robe on the box. Wind rough and sleet in it. Passengers snugging in straw inside to their chins and me stiffening like a board. Whiskey saved me. Bottle in my pocket and a nip every quarter mile. Licked the cold but the liquor got me. Went plumb asleep and might have piled somewhere except a passenger took over. Only a couple straight miles left so he did all right. Shook me awake so I could take it the last stretch and the Company not know. Finished the bottle. The two of us." That dry old chuckle followed. "Passenger named Tom Davisson. Young then but already had a jaw."

Sometimes things he said upset me. I could talk to him about the holdup and maybe I talked too much about it. I was always going over it in my mind and sticking on points that bothered me. "Uncle Ben," I said once. "Do you think I should've pulled out with the coach and maybe saved the gold?"

"Was Billy dead then?"

"Yes," I said. I couldn't have told how I knew. It was a feeling that had come to me there on the coach after I'd heard him fall and his gun stop shooting.

"And the man inside?" Uncle Ben said. "The drummer."

"Yes," I said. It was the same with him, a feeling after the scream and the following silence.

"You were right to stay," Uncle Ben said. "Race was alive and on the ground. He was more important than the gold. Persons are more important than things." And after a moment he said, "Suppose you had more passengers inside? A good chance some still kicking?"

"I don't know," I said. "I don't know what I'd have done."

"You'd have pulled out," Uncle Ben said. "Or should have." We jogged along and I could see what he meant but I couldn't decide what I really would have done so I jumped to another yet still somehow the same point. "Should Race have made me pull out when Billy told him to?"

"Yes. You still had the gold and a passenger and Billy was gone. Said so and knew."

"Would you?" I said.

Uncle Ben chewed on that. "Can't say. Would know I should. Can't say certain I would." We jogged along and after a while a kink eased out of my mind and I saw something plain. "Race couldn't," I said. "If he could, he wouldn't be Race." And after another while, "He wasn't thinking only of Billy."

Uncle Ben looked at me sharp and back at the horses' bobbing ears. "Some," he said. "Race was thinking of Billy some. Race is man all through. But thinking of himself too. Of being Race. Person people talk about. Tell tales about." We jogged along and Uncle Ben scrunched down lower on the seat and shook his head a little. "Ever think, Jess, why Race was just a messenger? With the Company a long time, longer'n Bowen. Still just a messenger. Never moved up to a job like Bowen's or any other. Never was moved up, that is."

"He's the best messenger on the whole line," I said.

"Yes," Uncle Ben said. "The best. Most of the time. But that's all." We jogged along and the ground began to rise so I let the horses slow to a walk and I was angry, I didn't know at what and I knew I shouldn't say it but I did all the same. "You've been with the Company a lot longer'n Race."

"Not talking about me," Uncle Ben said. He scrunched even lower on the seat and the horses plodded along and I began to feel ashamed and at last his voice came low, just a grumble in his throat. "Let a bum arm lick me too long."

He wouldn't say anything more and I couldn't think of anything fit to say and we were quiet all the rest of the way to the Gap.

It was the day of our third trip back to Goshen, that would be the sixth day after I returned to the Gap run, things started happening again. We had checked in at the station and Uncle Ben had squatted to checkers with the agent. I was on the porch thinking maybe I'd go see Russ Thorp again when Bowen called to me from his office. I went in and he shoved an envelope across the desk at me. "That'll clear you and some extra for a fair job," he said. "Today rounds out another month for you, Jess. It's a good stopping point. I've got someone to take your place."

That was too sudden for me to take without jolting. "Oh, you have, have you?" I said—"Certain have," he said. "Frank Hatt's boy Wes. He'll start tomorrow."—"Him?" I said. "He's just a kid. He can't drive."—"He's done some," Bowen said. "Everybody has to learn sometime. With Uncle Ben he'll learn fast."—"God damn it," I said. "I could drive better'n he ever will the day I came here and you stuck me on that same lousy run."—"It was the only spot I could place you," Bowen said. "Think I'd bounce one of the regulars just to shove in a cocky youngster? Believe it or not it's been doing you some good. Now you're too big for your britches and want to set them on somebody else's box. I'm letting you."

"Damn right," I said. "You and your whole goddam line couldn't stop me." I started out mad and had to turn back for the envelope and that made me madder and I stomped out on the porch and down to the street. Sure, I had been intending to leave and almost any time now and I had been saying I was going to leave, but having it pushed at me so sudden and so damn definite there couldn't be any changing made me mad. I guess being mad was a covering up for the hollow feeling low inside me. Bowen was calling my bluff and I hadn't realized till just then there was anything of a bluff to it and now there wasn't a thing left to do except go through with it.

I plowed up the street nursing my mad to keep my chin straight and myself from doing anything foolish and around the corner to Tom's office. He wasn't there. Dodd Burnett was on a chair tilted against the wall. He kept the office for Tom and tended the jail and was about right for that kind of work because he was a consumptive and couldn't do much of anything else. The job didn't pay much but he didn't need much, only for the medicines he kept getting by mail from Chicago. They didn't do him any good but he thought they did and he was always reading patent-medicine papers and planning what to send for next. He carried a smell around with him something like a drug shop, an old one with bottles left lying around open, and that bothered some people. Not Tom. A man that's dying by slow degrees, Tom said once, has a right to petrify himself with any kind of liquor he likes.

Burnett must have had a new one this time. There was a new edge on the smell, something like tar with a tinge of old peppermint. But I wasn't interested in that. "When's that judge due?" I said.

"Tomorrow," he said.

"How soon can we have the trial?" I said.

"The day after," he said. "If the judge's willing. He sets the docket. The sooner the better for my money." He jerked his head toward the back rooms. "That one's so guilty it's a waste of time. He should of been fanning the air days ago. Think I like keeping that murderer in my jail? Fixing his food. Carrying out his bucket. And him mean as—"

Burnett stopped talking. Tom Davisson was coming in the door. Tom nodded at me and made the swivel chair by his old rolltop squeak as he dropped into it. "Bowen's bounced me," I said. "Well, maybe not exactly. I was going to quit anyway and—" Tom shut me off with a flat hand up. "Sure. He told me this morning. Damn you, Jess, why do you have to be worrying me when I've got worries enough? Slater still loose and the judge coming and the Company hollering can't something be done about that gold."

"Seems to me," I said, "you're getting soft. Doing your worrying in a swivel chair. Why aren't you out ferreting for that Slater? Looks like you're letting Race do your work for you."

"Shut up," he said. He didn't say it mean or because he was peeved at what I was saying. He wanted me to shut up because someone was hurrying in the door, a tall lean gent who was puffing some and had his head pushed forward with a long nose thrust out.

"Name's Horner," this gent said. "My place's a piece off west of Halfway." A piece. I recognized him now. I'd seen him once or twice. He had a small ranch and it was all of seventeen-eighteen miles west of Halfway. He puffed on, fast as his breath would let him. "Don't get to town much. Don't like people. Had to come. Something you ought to know. Anything in it for me?"

"That depends," Tom said speaking careful, "on what you have to tell me."

"Won't tell if there isn't."

Suddenly Tom leaned forward and his chair squeaked once, short and shrill. "Is it about Slater?"

"Could be."

"How in hell," Tom said biting the words sharp, "can I know your information's worth a damn 'less you tell me? If you're smelling after a reward there ain't any. I've stopped the Company on that for a while so the hills won't be full of fools messing around and shooting each other's ears off. But if you've got anything, the Company'll be paying."

"You hear me mention reward?" this gent said. "No reward for doing my duty. It's my time. Three hours afogging in. Three hours the same home. Figure that's worth six bits."

Tom stared at him and you'd have thought Tom's jaw was going to drop off. Tom fished in a pocket and found the money and handed it to him. "About Slater?"

"Didn't say it was him. Just could be. Fellow stopped at my place this morning. Early. Walking. Bought a horse and a burro. Said he was a prospector heading for the gold country. Said his animals died and put him afoot. Said his pack was a piece away and he'd pick it up and be moving on. Didn't think it was funny till after he was gone a while."

"Funny?" Tom said.

"Right. Never argued about the prices. Paid cash. Never knew a prospector with cash. Never knew one used a horse. Always walk. Lead the burro. Didn't talk like one either. Clothes all right but not dirty enough. What's he doing way off the road? No gold around there. Road's the best way up to the gold country."

"Did he have a mustache?" I said.

"No. Not a whisker."

"He could've shaved," Tom said. "Matter of fact, he would've."

"Kind of yellowish complected?" I said.

"Brown. Reddish brown. Sort of heavy sunburn."

"He could've colored himself some," Tom said.

"Funnier yet," Horner said.

"Yes?" Tom and I said that together.

"Backtracked him. Not hard now he had the animals. Found where he'd been. No dead animals around. No signs he'd had any. Nice hideaway. Little cave. Food tins inside. Empty of course."

"Mr. Horner," Tom said. "You're a thorough man. Were you thorough enough to check which way he was heading?"

"Not born yesterday," Horner said. "Nor the day before that. He went west toward Old Mantrap. Hell of a big mountain that is. Probably going to climb the first ridge. There's a trail behind that. Found it once chasing cows. Old Indian trail. Corkscrews north somewheres."

Tom pushed out of his chair and went to a map on the wall. "Dodd," he said, tossing the words over his shoulder, "outside and saddle the black."

"Dodd," I said, "saddle another one."

Tom turned from the map and looked at me and I looked right back at him. "They took that gold from my coach," I said. Tom looked at me and I fidgeted my feet and then kept them firm on the floor. "Doing it my way again," I said. "I'm going along." Tom looked at me and his face was hard as always but I'd have sworn there was a hint of something different deep in his eyes. "Do it right then," he said. He jumped to the desk and yanked open a drawer and tossed me a deputy's badge and jumped back to the map. Dodd Burnett scuttled out the door and around the building and this gent Horner stood just inside and watched us. "Want me?" he said. "Cost no more'n my time."

"No," Tom said. "More people'd clutter the landscape. You'll oblige by not telling anyone else. Anything comes of it I'll see the Company keeps you in mind." All the time he was talking he was studying the map and buckling on his gunbelt and reaching for his hat without looking away from the map.

I pulled the gun out of the pocket of my jacket, my own jacket not the Company's this time, and held it out. "Got anything that'll fit this?" I said. I had cleaned and oiled it but it wasn't loaded. I hadn't been sure I'd ever want to shoot it. "It was Billy Skinner's," I said. Tom didn't seem to notice. "Bullets on the shelf," he said. But when I was reaching some down I felt his hand on my shoulder. "Billy was a good man," he said. "All the same you'll use it only if I say so." He wasn't asking me. He was telling me.

Horner watched us starting out the door. "Move fast, don't you," he said. We were swinging around the building when he called to us from the doorway. "Another thing. Horse he bought's a bay. Has big back feet. Shod it myself. Work-horse shoes. Double calks."

We were about eight miles out, heading due west. We were pushing the horses and had to stop by a stream to breathe them and let them take on a little water. "We aren't going this blind, are we, Tom?" I said. "You must have something figured."

"If Horner's telling the truth," he said, "and there's no reason he shouldn't, that trail snakes along the base of the big mountains on there behind the first line of high ridge. That's lonesome country. Never been there myself. It figures by the time we reach it Slater—if it's Slater and he'll be moving fast—will be about where we'll hit it coming across straight like this. We'll head him or pick up his tracks fairly close."

We hammered on, due west, taking the hills we were coming into straight on, not trying to skirt around them, bee-lining direct for the spot Tom had picked on his map. We came to the high ridge that ran forty miles or more, a high sharp barrier in front of the mountains. We started up it and the horses had to dig in, scrambling step by step upward and weaving through the scrub growth. "Tom," I said, "what if it's the wrong man?"—"It won't be," he said. "Feel it in my bowels like I have before. We'll get him and the gold and we'll wrap it so tight in court nobody'll be trying to stop a coach in my district again."

We reached the top and dropped down the other side enough to be out of sight against the sky and stopped and dismounted. The horses needed that. They stood with heads hanging and legs quivering and the funny thought hit me as it did sometimes, what a stupid or a wonderful thing a horse was that it'd beat itself against time and distance and any difficult job and give all it had and keep going till it dropped if a man wanted it to. "He's smart," Tom said suddenly. "So goddamn smart it could scare you." I kept quiet and he talked on, sort of thinking this out for himself too. "When he's near his hideout he chucks his horse so it'll be harder to track him there. That takes cold nerve but he has that. Lugs the gold and his saddle the rest of the way himself.

When he figures the hoorawing has died away some, he slips
out to buy another horse. Picks a lone-wolf rancher he thinks
is dumb. That's his one mistake and that'll throw him. But
everything else is perfect. He adds the burro to help his
disguise and make carrying the gold easier. Suppose somebody sees him. Just another prospector wandering around
the way they do. He'll ease up into the gold country, the
opposite direction most people expect him to go. He'll find
some diggings and take a claim and make a show of mining.
Nobody'll suspect anything when he begins to have gold to
ship. Hell, he'll even have the Company shipping the gold
he's stolen from them."

Tom started down the slope leading his horse and I followed and we found that bad going because it was steep and
the horses might come slipping down on us so we mounted
and picked our way down with the horses moving slow, front
legs stiffened, with their rumps almost sliding. The slope
eased out and we came to the level and we were in a long
twisting valley like a huge sluiceway running south and north
with the upper end crags of Old Mantrap climbing big and
formidable and merging into the next in the range on one
side and the high blunt edge of the ridge on the other. It
was beautiful country, beautiful in the hard rugged honesty
of the great timeless rock formations, but it was forbidding
country and you could see why it was lonesome country,
and the level and more fertile land around Goshen and the
rolling hills between would have to be well filled before people would be coming into it.

A rocky, dry stream bed ran through the valley where
in thaw time or heavy rains water must have raced and
tossed the stones like a kid playing with pebbles. On the
other side of this, following it but a hundred feet or more
away and on higher ground, we found the trail. You could
stand in the stirrups and look forward and back and make
it out, a thin trace through the coarse grass and scrub bushes
and thorn thickets, almost overgrown in places and showing
plain in others, and the long reach of it discernible in the
distant perspective. You could tell it was there too in the
feel underfoot, the harder packing of the ground. No one
would ever know for how many centuries animals had used
it and after them or with them wandering Indians and later
perhaps at rare intervals the first of the white men pene-
trating into the territory and looking for a pass beyond the

mountains. Now in the whole stretching sweep within the
scope of our eyes there was nothing to show that anyone,
any person, had ever lived or moved in that region, nothing
except the thin broken tracery of that trail marking its way
into the distance, twisting with every twist of the dry stream
bed and disappearing where the valley turned out of sight
far ahead.

"Someday there'll be a road here," I said. "And people
moving on it and coaches rolling. Someday maybe I'll drive
it."

"Someday's not today," Tom said. "Only one man moving
on it we're interested in today. Come along." And we ranged
alongside that trail studying every yard of it and in the first
soft spot we found the prints, not many but enough, a few
faint of the delicate little hoofmarks of a burro and several
of a horse, one deep enough and distinct. Even from the
saddle we could see them, the double-calk indentations. Tom
swung down and felt the edges with his fingers and crumbled
some of the dirt. "At least an hour," he said. "He's moving
fast." Tom swung up and we lined out along that trail at a
good clip.

Fast and slow, that was the way we went, the same
thing over and over, fast when we had an open stretch ahead,
slow when we were rounding a turn and wondering what
might be in sight, then fast again when we saw the trail
clear. Every now and then we'd slow too when we'd hit a
soft stretch to check for the hoofprints, slowing just enough
to see if they were there and pushing on. After four or five
miles something began bothering me and I wasn't sure about
it and then we passed a soft spot and I reined around and
called to Tom. He circled back, pulling down his eyebrows
and ready to lay into me, and I just pointed at the ground.
He reined his horse in sharp and looked down and, stopped
like that, he could see what I had noticed. Prints were there
all right. The little ones of the burro. The big double calks
of the horse. And others, smaller but not too small, with
the single calks showing clear. "Yes," I said. "There's another one. Where in hell did he come from?" Tom didn't
bother to answer. He couldn't have known any more than
I did. This second man had come out of nowhere or out of
anywhere along the way we were traveling, dropping out
of the sky or down the ridge and swinging in on the trail
somewhere to add his prints to the others.

Tom swung down and felt the edges. "They're not together," he said. "His are fresher. But not much."

"You think he's following too," I said, "or just riding the trail?"

Tom shook his head. "We'll know soon. They're not far ahead now." He mounted and started on and he hadn't said or done a thing to show he was worried about this other man but I noticed he was riding faster and I had to make my horse hump to keep fairly close behind him.

Suddenly the air was different. There was a chill in it and the light was changing. The sun had gone behind the mountains. In a little while dusk would be creeping around us and I was wondering whether Tom would keep right on into the dark when I had to rein in quick or run into him. He was stopping and swinging down. I did too and saw the prints. The burro and the double-calk had turned off the trail here and headed up the slope to the left. You could see where the single-calk horse had stopped and stamped a bit while whoever was on him studied the ground and where his prints too headed off to the left. "He's following," I said. I was talking to myself. Tom was walking away, leading his horse, bending over to catch the prints in the coarse grass. It didn't make sense, that jog to the left, because the slope just climbed a couple hundred feet to a small hill flat-top with the mountain wall rising sheer behind it. I hurried to follow Tom and we had climbed near the cliff when he motioned to me to stop. I heard the noise then, a rustling in the bushes close by the rock. I reached quick for my gun and Tom had his ready too and we went forward slow, bug-eyed with watching the bushes, and Tom called out and there was nothing, not a sound of any kind around us. "Wait here," Tom said and dropped his reins and went forward, crouching and trying to peer into the bushes, and disappeared among them. I waited and my nerves were crawling and I was ready to shoot anything that moved when I heard his voice. Just the one word, short and disgusted. "Damn!" He came out holding the frayed end of a rope and pulled and out after him came a flop-eared burro.

"Rest of the stuff's in there," Tom said. "Usual prospector things. He did it up right. This thing here scraped the pack off against the rock."

"The gold?" I said.

"No," Tom said. "Took that with him."

We searched around and the prints told the story. Slater had cut off up there for something or other, maybe a rest, and to check the trail behind him. He had clear view from that flattop of maybe a mile. He'd seen the second rider coming and cut loose the burro because he couldn't make the best time with it and slapped the gold on his horse and lit out full speed, hugging close to the cliff wall so the hill would hide him for a while and not let the rider coming know he was so close. We found the prints where that second rider learned that too and took out ahelling with the single-calks digging deep alongside the double-calks.

"What'd he do that for?" I said. "Slater. He was set to fool most anybody with his prospector dodge."—"What do you think?" Tom said.—"Well," I said, "maybe he got panicky."—"He did that all right," Tom said.—"But why?" I said. "The way he's pulled things so far he's not the kind to panic easy."—"But he did," Tom said. "It figures he recognized who's following and got scared." Tom looked at me and wiped a hand across his face and down under his chin and along his neck and looked at me like he wanted to say something and couldn't quite do it. "I'd be scared too," he said.

"Who?" I said. And then I knew. There was only one man would be riding lonesome country like that, day after day, endless and untiring, searching out the hidden places and following every strange track he found. There was only one man could put a panic in a cold planner like Slater by the mere sight of him following. But I couldn't say the name either. I could just stare at Tom and watch the knowledge bite into him and then he was leaping on his horse and lifting it into a gallop and leaning low along its neck to try to see the prints rushing past him.

Try as I would I couldn't catch up with him. I could hold my own and that was all. We tore along by the cliff and around a sharp curve and down to the relative level of the trail again and on along its thin tracery through the fading light. Then the long narrow valley widened and embraced a sudden stand of gnarled trees by a pool and the floor of the valley beyond rose sharp and broke into rocky draws twisting and climbing on every side with great tumbled stones in them. We pulled up short in the trees and stopped, panting, and the swift dusk of the mountains caught us, dropping like a soft blanket enveloping us and everything around us and turning the big jagged rock formations ahead into great grotesque chunks of dark shadow.

We sat our saddles quiet and listening and we were the only living things in that strange country. The prints we had been following were not real. They were only the ghostly legacy of some far-off time, coming out of nowhere and disappearing into the same, and we were isolated and alone. But there was a burro back down the valley. We had seen it. Tom had pulled it on a rope. Perhaps it too had disappeared now, fading out into the darkness that was taking the world. And then, above and ahead of us, lost in the far deep shadows, a stone moved and rolled, bouncing and clattering. The sounds, sharp and distinct, drifted down to us and died away and our ears ached with the strain of listening in the silence. Then, farther above and ahead, a horse whinnied and was cut short as if someone had clamped its nose and a gun spoke and was answered and spoke again and a horse screamed and its hooves beat against rock. The sounds shook down through the draws, repeating themselves in dying echoes, and sank away and the silence returned and stretched forward and we sat quiet in our saddles and hearing nothing.

Tom swung down, landing soft and springy, and dropped his reins. I did the same. "Keep it quiet," he whispered. "Maybe he heard us coming. But he doesn't know where we are."

"Who?" I said.

"Slater," he said. "Maybe we can work around above him." He caught me by the arm. "If you have to shoot, aim low. For the legs. We want him alive." He started up through the rocks to the left, stepping careful to avoid loose stones, and I followed. It was a fool thing to do because there was another man up there somewhere, a man who could shoot the pips out of a deuce of spades at fifty paces while just about anybody else would still be only thinking of drawing a bead and who would be shooting now at anything that moved. We climbed awhile, our guns ready in our hands, and got about halfway to the wide spine of rock that topped the draws and ran across between the mountain and the high ridge. Tom was a bit ahead of me and I hurried some and stepped on a small stone that rolled under my foot and threw me. It was lucky I went down because the instant that stone scraped the ground a shot sliced the silence like a knife cutting and a bullet whined over me from the right to smash into the rocks beyond me. And in the next instant Tom shouted, one word, the name we had been unable to speak. "Race!" And he flung himself flat and another shot, this time from above us, caught the echoes of the first and the bullet went ricocheting down the slope.

Silence again, empty and waiting. And then into it came a voice from the right, familiar and nerve-tingling. "Damn your hide, Tom. I should have known it'd be you. Who's your friend?"

"It's me. Jess," I said and the voice came again.

"The kid too. Getting to be quite a reunion here in these rocks. Come on over. Don't mind that bastard up there. He won't shoot again because he knows I'll have him placed."

We scrambled across, keeping low behind rocks, and found him behind a big one, big enough to shelter him and his horse, which was standing a few feet from him. He was leaning against the low end of the rock staring into the blackness up the slope and he didn't even turn his eyes away to look at us as we came close. His right hand lay on top of the rock holding a revolver and I shuddered a bit at the thought of the instant snap deadliness that could leap from that hand at any sound in the night.

"How'd you get on to him?" Tom whispered and Race chuckled, grim and rumbling in his throat.

"What in hell you whispering for? Let the bastard hear. He's dead before morning and he knows it. He had to be in this territory somewhere. I'd combed out the rest. Came over the ridge some miles back and found his tracks. The little jack fooled me for a time but thought I'd run them down on the off chance. When he spotted me and went loco I was about sure. When I got in here and caught a whiff of him I knew it. Don't have to see what he looks like to know. My guts tell me it's him."

"It's him all right," Tom said. "We even know where he hid out."

"No hiding for him now," Race said. "I've got him cold. Knocked over his horse a few minutes ago. Too dark to smoke him out yet but he's penned tight. Can't go over the top or he'll show plain against the sky. Can't get up the sides. Too steep and he'd be a sitting duck. Can't get down around without me hearing him move. Soon as the moon's up I go get him."

"We get him," Tom said.

"No," Race said. "This is my play. You'll want to baby him and take him to your damned court. This time it's going to be my way."

"Maybe," Tom said. "Maybe he'll force it to that."

"Right." I jumped at the sound of that voice above us lost somewhere in the dark rocks, unmistakable, the voice I'd heard at the Hatt House and again from the stable at Big Creek. "You'll not take me alive. You'll not take me at all. Make a move up this way and I'll blast you back down."

Tom didn't seem to hear him and Race just kept staring up the slope. "Jess," Tom said. "Keep your eye peeled on that skyline. If anything shows sing out and we'll all start blasting." He put a hand on Race's shoulder. "You've been going it hard for days, Race. Ease off while we're waiting. I've got the makings." He moved over where the rock loomed bigger and leaned against it and took out his tobacco pouch and papers and rolled a cigarette. Race pushed out from the rock and turned his head slow to watch the tiny flame cupped in Tom's hands flicker with Tom's breath and be blown out. He moved close to Tom and reached and Tom handed him the makings and he rolled his own and lit it. Side by side they leaned against the rock and their voices floated out to fade away into the clear dark purity of the night.

"All men make mistakes," Tom said. "You ride yourself too hard over yours."

"So you know," Race said.

"Yes. I know what's been eating you. You feel responsible. You talked too much."

That's right." Again Slater's voice joined in. "The big blowhard tipped me."

I thought Race would flare at that but he didn't. He didn't pay any attention to Slater at all. Neither of them did. For all you could tell they didn't know there was anyone in the world but themselves. "It's always the same," Race said. "I talk too much. Too often. I can't help it. I try to make up for it in other ways."

"When a mistake's made, Race, it's made. You can't wipe it out. Not even with blood. You have to learn to live with it. We both know that."

"My God, Tom, there's more. More than you could understand. This time they got away with it. Billy and one of

the tenders and that passenger. And the gold. They busted
my record and—"

"You're holy hell right we did." Slater's voice was harsh
and mocking, a weird sound striking down out of the night.
"That was about the best part of it. You thought it couldn't
be done. Well, I did it."

Race had paused. He didn't seem to be listening, only
waiting. "But they didn't do it really. I did it. Maybe this
won't make sense but I keep thinking and thinking when
they're all dead it'll be better. It'll be squared some."

"It makes sense to me," Tom said. "But they'll be just
as dead when they're hung by court order as if you threw
lead into them. And you won't have to go around thinking
maybe you shot when there wasn't a real need for it. That's
worse. That's murder, a kind of murder, and I know too
damn well how it can live inside you and gnaw at you in
your bunk at night. My court can kill as thorough as your
guns when killing's the proper answer. Can you see that,
Race?"

"Maybe," Race said. "Maybe not. My gun's been a damn
good answer plenty times and you know it. It's certain. And
it's mine." Race drew on his cigarette and let the smoke out
slow and Tom began talking, easy and steady like he was
thinking of things that meant a lot to him and were right
ready to come out. "Remember, Race. Remember the time
we were both young and full of juice and I rode line camp
and like a fool got lost in a blizzard and near froze. Who was
it brought me in?"

"I did," Race said. "You were stiff as a poker. Damn
heavy too."

"Remember Dicey Burren selling watered whiskey in
that flea-coop of his? When he got caught sliding aces off
the bottom of the deck, who was it threw him and his friends
out the windows and had a hell of a time shooting the bottles
off the shelves?"

"We did," Race said. "You and me."

"Remember when you were jugged for disturbing the
peace when all you were doing was shooting a few street
lamps and you got to hiccuping and the justice told you to
quit and you couldn't so he fined you for contempt of court
and you got mad and told him you'd show him what contempt
was and near pulled his beard off. Who was it bailed you

out and helped you finish the street lamps before leaving town?"

"You did," Race said. "Damn your hide. You did."

"And one time I was stuck behind an upturned table in Murray's old place with three cattle thieves behind the bar clipping my hair every time I wiggled and everybody else was hightailing for the next county. Who was it popped off a moving coach outside and looked in and said, 'Having a little trouble, Tom?' and stood there in the open spraying lead so fast and accurate they tossed out their guns and crawled out to be jailed?"

"Guess that was me," Race said. "Seem to remember something like that. I know what you're doing, Tom. You're working on me. But that's all right. We've seen a few things together that're maybe worth remembering."

"Well, then, you goddam son of an off-color mule, what are we two doing out here on the edge of this country we've helped give a little notion of how to behave decent, talking about your way and my way when we both know there's only one way to wind this up right and that's to take him still kicking and get the gold out of him if it's hid somewhere and turn him over to the court for a proper hanging?"

Nothing moved anywhere along the skyline I was watching and the edge of it began to be tipped with faint silver and the moon inched, slow and reluctant, over the ridge on the right. Out of the corner of my eye I saw the spurt of Race's match as he lit another cigarette and pulled long on it and Tom's voice went on, quiet and steady. "You heard him, Race. That bastard up there thinks we can't do it. You and me, Race. He thinks we can't do it." And still Race said nothing and the silence grew and the moon came clear of the ridge top and the whole twisted tormented slope we were on became a sheen of shimmering gray, weird and broken with the dark pools of rock shadow. And Tom's voice came again, whispering now, "There ain't been any comment from up there for a while now."

He and Race were beside me, peering over the low end of the big rock. The silence was a dead thing and no man lived in it but the three of us peering into it in the pale light of the moon. "Stay here, Jess," Tom whispered, "and hold the middle. Race, you take the left there. I'll swing out to the right. We'll work up on him." And still Race said nothing. He just slipped away to the left and Tom did to the right and they were lost in the shadows and I was alone in my own dark pool by our rock.

I waited and I could hear nothing, not even one of them, and I forgot all caution and climbed up on the big rock and stood tall to look around. Way over to the left by the cliff wall I heard a snitch of sound or saw a small blur of movement, I wasn't sure which except that my attention was caught there and then I saw him. It could only be Slater, sliding from shadow pool to shadow pool, and he was below us, working down to where we had left the horses.

"Tom!" I shouted. "Race! He's by the cliff! Heading for the horses!" The instant I shouted the silence was broken by more than my words. A shot from Slater slashed at me and went wide and then he was not bothering to shoot. He was running, still moving from rock cover to rock cover, but running and not caring whether he made noise. Race and Tom, farther up the slope, were running too and stones were rolling and the clatter was echoing back and forth between the mountain and the ridge. As I swung my head I could see all three of them in flashes, jumping jacks bobbing among the rocks, Slater down and near the bottom of the slope and Race and Tom up and coming abreast of me on either side. Then Tom hit a stretch of what must have been loose shale and water-worn stones and he went flat and was rolling with the rubble clattering around him and it was Race alone who was driving down in great leaps, gaining steadily. But not fast enough. Slater was almost at the bottom and in another moment would be in the clear and into the trees where the horses were.

And then Race did it.

There's not another man ever lived could have done it. He was leaping down and down, stumbling on the uncertain footing and catching himself and driving down, a big leaping shape with the moonlight shining on his hair with the black jagged scar across it, and Slater was just a blur of darkness seen in snatches between the tumbled rocks. And I saw Race's gun flash almost in the midst of a leap, flash in that terrible snap deadliness that was like a snake striking, and Slater pitched forward into a patch of moonlight and rolled into a shadow pool and was still.

Tom and I went down the slope together leading Race's horse. We found Race standing by the crumpled body. His gun was in its holster and his arms were folded across his

chest and he was breathing deep and regular. His eyes were
burning in the moonlight but not in little leaping flames. The
fire in them was deep and steady. "There's your man," he
said to Tom. "Knocked out. Banged his head on that stone.
I took him in the leg." He looked straight at Tom and his
face was as hard now as Tom's with the same enduring flint.
"Your court better be quick and sure with him or I'll never
play it your way again."

We only had three horses and there were four of us. The
other horse, the one with the double calks, was lying dead
up the slope among the rocks. That meant somebody would
have to walk and the somebody couldn't be Slater, not with
a wounded leg, a bullet hole in the thigh about four inches
above the knee. Tom bandaged it best he could while Slater
was still unconscious. When he was able to sit up and take
notice we put him on one of the three horses and ran a piece
of rope between his feet under the horse's belly just in case
and to help hold him on and put a lead rope on the bridle.
We put the saddlebags over the withers in front of him,
those with the gold in them, all the rest of it, about eighty
pounds of it. We found them, Race and I, while Tom was
doing the bandaging. They were stashed between two good-
sized stones and smaller stones had been laid around to cover
the opening. Slater must have had his trouble moving those
stones in the dark without making a sound we could hear.
And the dark fooled him. He missed one end of a strap that
was sticking out and showed in the moonlight. In a sense,
though, that was lucky for him. If we'd had trouble finding
it we would've had to work him over to make him talk. And
the way he was acting he wouldn't have talked easy. He
wasn't doing any talking at all. He sat slumped in the saddle,
leaning a little to favor the bad leg, and kept his mouth shut.

He wasn't much sitting there in the moonlight. About
medium size with some flesh around the waist and thin shoulders. He had sharp, kind of pointed features and his face
was hatchet-shaped, the kind of a face that ought to be easy
to remember. But if it hadn't been for the voice coming down
the slope awhile before and the gold and the way everything
fitted, I wouldn't have recognized him. All I could really
remember about how he looked was the sallowness of his
face and the mustache. That's how it is when there's a person
doesn't impress you much and no matter how many times

you see him about sort of casual passing all you remember is one or two things that catch your eye. With that mustache gone and his clothes different and his skin darkened I could have been right close to him and not known him. As Tom said, he was a smart one. That mustache had been one of his smartest tricks.

"We'll take spells walking," Tom said and pulled three blades of grass. "Short one starts." I got the short one and we began the return trip, Tom leading with the extra saddle from the dead horse on the withers in front of him and Race following with Slater in tow and me hiking in the rear. We went a short way back along the trail then Tom struck off to the left straight to the high ridges and up it. That was tough going for the horses but tougher for me with only two legs and no hooves on them. Tom pulled over and slowed till I was beside him. "Take hold of the tail," he said. "Try a pull." I took hold of his horse's tail and that black horse went along with me worrying it like that and never once tried to kick me loose. We topped the ridge and stopped. Race swung down. "Climbing that counts for quite a distance," he said. "Reckon it's my turn." I was mighty glad to get my feet off the ground and my rump on that saddle. And Tom stared out over the rolling hills and got his bearings though I couldn't see how in the dim half-light of the moon and we started down the other side of the ridge with Race walking.

We were moving slow, our pace cut to match Race's legs, and there was plenty of time for thinking. I was feeling good. Tired but good. I'd think of Slater on the horse behind me at the other end of the lead rope tied to my saddlehorn and I'd wonder how such an insignificant sort of a man as he now seemed could have been the cause—maybe not the whole cause because he was only part of the whole vast interlocking web of people impinging on people and events upon them too with the bad strands meshed with the good and the accidents of evil smashing out of it and suddenly being there to be seen though the possibility of them was always there too only hidden—how he could have been the cause, the immediate pushing cause of the violence that had flared into the night at Big Creek. But I didn't wonder too much about that. Because we were making an end to it. Maybe not a final and complete end because I was beginning to see that nothing men did ever had a final and complete end, the effects going on in many and indefinable and often untraceable ways, if only in the memories of those left living. But we were making a kind of end. Slater was on the horse behind me, and the gold too. In a matter of days, maybe hours, the court would take care of him and the other man already in Tom's jail. Billy was dead and a drummer whose name I didn't even know, but that part was over. The bitter was done and we were making an end. And how could I feel anything but good? Slater was nothing now. He was out of it. He was finished. He was not really there any more. I was traveling through a clean sweet night with the two men who were like two parts of me, bigger and wider and deeper than I would ever be, but parts of me, and they had been pulling me in opposite directions because they had been moving away from each other, driven along their own separate and inevitable paths by the necessity that resides in its own form in every moving man, and now they were together again and I was with them. I had heard and seen. I had heard them while they let me keep watch and took for granted I would watch right, two men, articulate yet inarticulate, reaching out for each other with words about the past that they were applying to the present. I had heard Tom Davisson plead in the only way he could, not directly but with memories. I had seen Race Crim respond in the only way he could, not with words but at the crucial moment with the instant flash of will that deflected his gun muzzle down. They were together now, hard-faced and silent but together, and I was with them, one of them and sharing in what they were doing, and I felt good.

We had spelled each other twice over and the moon was low behind us when a batch of buildings grew out of the ground ahead of us and we went past a couple of sheds and stopped by a small house. Tom dismounted and went to the door and hammered on it with his gun butt. He waited and nothing happened and Tom hammered again and a window to one side of the door opened a couple of inches and a voice wavered at him. "Got a shotgun here. Loaded too."

"Petey, you old fool," Tom said. "It's me. Tom Davisson."

"Why'nt you say so?" the voice said and the window went down and the door opened and an old man in a nightshirt and skull cap peered out. "Goldurndest time to come visiting. But there's coffee left in the pot and I'll—" He saw us and popped out of sight and reappeared with the shotgun. "Tom, get in quick. A passel o' thieves out there."

"Only one," Tom said, "and he's tied harmless. I'm needing four fresh horses. Be leaving three here. We'll straighten out in a day or two."

"Horses?" the old man said. "Take 'em. Anything you want, Tom. Catch 'em yourself though. Ain't gettin' me out in any night air. Poisonous." I expect he realized he was breathing some of the poison because he slammed the door and Tom waved to us and led around the house to a pole corral in back.

There wasn't much pick among the horses there but at least they were fresh and we all could be mounted. We moved along faster now and Tom kept us at a steady trot. We were getting into level land and color began to streak up the sky ahead and a little to the left and the sun jumped over the horizon and fought awhile with the late moon way over nearly opposite and then the moon faded to a vague circle of white and dropped away behind the hills. In the morning clear I began to recognize the country around. Finally we hit the road swinging in from the Gap and we turned right to follow it and headed toward Goshen. We knocked off the miles, steady and not slowing, and something like a crawling bug grew in the road far ahead and kept growing and became the old coach with Uncle Ben Nunan on the box and beside him, holding the reins, young Wes Hatt. We could see them plain a long stretch before we reached them and I was feeling good enough to admit open to myself that young Wes seemed to be doing all right with the ribbons. He was maybe holding those old horses in too tight and playing with the leather too much because they didn't need attention and could walk that road in their sleep but he was doing all right.

They stopped and we did too and for a moment a lot of talk was flipping back and forth with me maybe doing too much when Uncle Ben cut it short. "Tom, better take that man in quick as you can."

We all stared at him, even Slater, and that was the first time Slater had shown any sign of giving a damn about what went on around him. "Been moving along," Tom said. "Haven't stopped for a wink of sleep. Anything new?"

"Judge pulled in last night," Uncle Ben said. "A hustler. Big circuit he has. You hurry."

Tom and Race looked at each other and the lines in their faces tightened and Race shrugged his shoulders and looked away and Tom swung his horse and yanked on the lead rope to Slater's horse and started on and Race and I followed. We moved even faster now, fast as we could and hold a pace with those horses, and I noticed that Slater was sitting straighter in his saddle and I began to nurse a worry inside me without knowing about what.

It was near ten-thirty pushing toward eleven when we rode into Goshen, past the station and up the street and around the corner to Tom's office. A lot of people were in sight, plenty more than usual. A dozen or more wagons and buggies were lined along the street and horses were tied to rails all along the way. Nobody noticed us much at first but by the time we were rounding the corner people were shouting after us and hurrying along the plank sidewalks to follow. We went straight to Tom's office and dismounted. Dodd Burnett was standing in the doorway. He stepped out to take care of the horses when Tom told him to and we lifted Slater down and Tom and I took him between us and Race hoisted the saddlebags and we went in. Someone else was already in there, more than one, two of them.

Judge Webb was there, Judge Lucius T. Webb, sitting in Tom's chair by Tom's desk, leaning back with the heels of his hands resting on the black cloth of the buttoned frock coat covering his plump stomach and the fingertips pressed together. He was a short man, short and plump, but you never thought of him as short and his plumpness was the solid kind all over that never made you think of him being soft and fat. He had a big head that settled down between his shoulders with plenty of steel-gray hair and a forehead that pushed out over his eyes and a big nose and a stiff cropped black mustache and a chin that showed he always knew his own mind. He had a presence that could fill a courtroom whether that was just a converted empty store like ours at Goshen or a dignified special-built place in one of the big towns way down the main line. You could tell the kind of man he was by the fact that when people talked about him they almost always used his full name.

At a small table against the wall near him was his clerk, back to us and writing, a thin little wisp of a bald-headed man whose name I never could remember if I'd ever even heard it. He wasn't really a man. He was a machine, a writing and recording machine. Wherever Judge Webb was, there he was too, satchel in hand, taking paper and pen out of it and waiting to start recording if the judge waggled a finger for that.

Judge Webb nodded at us and the clerk turned his head to see us and returned to his writing and that was all. Race dropped the saddlebags on the floor and shoved them aside with his foot and closed the door and stood with his back to it. Tom and I took Slater right through and to the jail part of the building and left him on the bunk in the cell next to the one already occupied by the other prisoner. We went forward to the office and Tom tossed his hat in a corner and sat down on the only remaining chair. "Jess," Tom said, "go find somebody can fix that leg better'n I did. Don't give a damn who."

That was a tough one because the only doctor we had yet around Goshen was about as hard to find as a flea on a long-haired dog. He didn't have an office, said he carried that around in his pocket. You had to hunt for him. He'd be at one of the bars cadging drinks or sleeping off those he'd already had in any place unexpected. I didn't want to go hunting, not right then, but Tom said to go so I went. I hesitated just long enough to hear Judge Webb start speaking.

"Mister Davisson," I heard him say and that struck me as a bad start because Judge Lucius T. Webb never forgot anyone he met once and used people's first names when he wasn't presiding in a courtroom and he knew Tom about as well as he knew anyone. "Mister Davisson. I trust you have a satisfactory explanation of your absence when you knew I was arriving for duty today."

Race opened the door and I stepped out and had to shove my way through people asking questions. I shouted answers at them and they were really buzzing when I pulled through and went around the corner to the main street. The first person I saw there was Luke Bowen. He was striding along, head out and eager. "Have they got it?" he said.

"It," I said. "And him." And because I couldn't help it I said something more and emphasized the first word. "*We* got them," I said. He looked sharp at me and hurried past and I was wondering which direction to take first when I saw something that made me feel lucky. It was a goatee bobbing along the plank sidewalk across the street attached to a plump little gent who was intimately acquainted with my person. "Doc," I called and Doc Schlegel stopped and I ran across to him. "Hey," I said, "what're you doing here?"

"Morning, Mister Harker," he said. "They might want me as a corroborating witness so I came along. That is just an excuse. Like to be where things are doing."

"Well, I've got you another bandaging job."

"What portion of your anatomy this time?" he said.

"Me?" I said. "I'm better'n new. It's Slater at the jail."

"Slater?" he said, eyes beaming. "Wonderful. Hope he has a nice collection of complicated bullet holes."

"Just one," I said. "In the leg."

"Let me not question sudden gifts," he said. "One will have to do. Lead on, my boy."

That man could make anyone feel warm and friendly toward the world and I was proud of getting a real doctor and quick, so I was shocked when we reached the office and went in. It was a pleasant day outside and the people out there were buzzing with excitement but inside you could feel the chill and stiffness in the air. Race was leaning against the wall, his eyes narrowed, his face flat without expression. Bowen was standing spraddle-legged over the saddlebags looking pleased and a bit puzzled as if he thought maybe he oughtn't to be pleased. The judged hadn't moved but his eyes were closed and he was tapping his fingertips together. His clerk had stopped writing and turned his chair and was waiting, a bald-headed wisp of a statue. And Tom was sitting forward in his chair staring at the judge and the vitality seemed to have oozed out of him and he was the tiredest man I'd ever seen.

Doc Schlegel blinked around at them. Nothing could hold that man down. "What's wrong in here?" he said. "Your star actor died so you can't jerk him through a trial?"

Tom stood up. "He's alive. Maybe too damn much alive." He led Schlegel back to the jail room and in the quiet their fading footsteps sounded strange and hollow. No one said a word and then Tom was standing in the inner doorway. "Judge," he said, "you're a damn fool."

Judge Webb's eyes opened and his fingers stopped their tapping. "Mister Davisson, from your immediate point of view, perhaps yes, so I will let that pass. As I told you, I am pressed for time. One day is my limit here until later this month."

"God damn it!" Tom shouted. "That's plenty. We can slap it through this afternoon. It's an open and shut case."

"No case is open and shut," Judge Webb said, not moving. "Not to an honest judge's mind before the testimony is given. This whole situation supports my contention that the policy of letting a sheriff also act as prosecutor in a district like this is a poor one. When I arrived you were off acting in your capacity as sheriff. You were not here to help me in your capacity as prosecutor. I had to take the liberty of going through your papers and preparing my own docket. I can clean it this afternoon. A few land-title cases and the usual drunk and disorderly. Word has been sent to the proper parties to appear. Now you hurry in and wish to add another, a serious case that must be handled properly. It cannot in the time available."

"What about the one we already had jugged?" Tom said. "You've got the papers on him. We just double it. Slide Slater in too."

"Ah, yes," Judge Webb said. "I wondered about him. I decided to bind him over till my next visit here. I see no reference that you have obtained a lawyer for his defense. And there is the matter of impaneling a jury."

"A lawyer?" Tom said. "He doesn't need a lawyer. He doesn't want one. No jury either. He'll plead guilty."

"Will he?" Judge Webb said. "Can you guarantee he will when we arraign him? Can you do the same for this new one? This Slater?" The words lingered in the air and Tom said nothing and came into the room and sank on his chair again and Judge Webb leaned forward, his weight squeaking the swivel chair. "Tom. You can not short circuit the legal process. You have two men out there charged with murder. A list of other charges too, but it boils down to that. You and those who have helped you have done a fine job getting them here for the law to handle. There have been entirely too many instances of summary so-called justice in this territory. We need some examples like this. The law will handle them. In due time. And by due process. They may be so plain guilty that the stench from them offends a decent man's nostrils. Somehow scoundrels like that seem always to be involved when the issue is put straight to us humans trying to do our best as we see it. But they are entitled to their day in court. They are entitled to a legal defense and a judging by a jury of their peers. They shall have it. And that requires time."

"A nice speech." That was Doc Schlegel in the inner doorway, rocking on his feet and no longer a cheery little man but a very serious one. "So nice and judicial it stinks. It might fit a settled civilized city back east somewheres. Not this country. Not yet."

"And will you tell me, Doctor Schlegel," Judge Webb said, his level voice not changing, "how this country is to be civilized if we do not make it so?"

"Theory," Doc Schlegel said. "Damn theory. It's not a theory I've been bandaging back there. It's a particularly loathsome kind of creature the judicial mind might make the mistake of calling a man. Stop thinking about him. Think about the people outside here who have been coming into town expecting a quick trial and a healthy hanging. They won't take kindly to any delay."

Judge Webb leaned back in the swivel chair and put his fingertips together again. "Always the practical man, are you not, Doctor Schlegel? Very well. Let me be practical too. Grant for the sake of argument a certain necessity to convict these men and hang them promptly. I let you rush me into doing it without the proper formalities—which are not really formalities but protections for each and every one of us in the event we ourselves tangle with the law. I speak the word and you hang them. They are very satisfactorily dead. But the issue is not. My decisions are still subject, and rightly so, to review by the higher courts. There is a finding that I acted summarily without regard to those—I will use the word again—those formalities. I stand discredited. What is worse the law itself stands discredited in this territory. What, then, have we actually accomplished?"

"Plenty." That was Luke Bowen. "We've shown every road agent who might get tricky notions what can happen to anyone tampers with one of my coaches."

"You too, Mister Bowen." Judge Webb sat in Tom's chair, unmoving and immovable. "Your gold has been regained. I might have thought that would temper your enthusiasm for hasty action."

"The gold be damned," Luke Bowen said. "They killed Billy Skinner."

"And a passenger," Doc Schlegel said. "That's sticking in people's minds. An innocent bystander, so to speak. Feeling is beginning to run strong. With Slater here now the public temperature will be rising."

"I will not compromise my convictions." Judge Webb's voice dropped a note or two and he seemed to be stiffening all over. "I will not be stampeded into an action we would all regret. You raise another point, Doctor Schlegel. How could I obtain an impartial jury here with everyone already convinced in advance? It may even be that I will have to order a change of venue, take this case to another part of the territory."

"Lucius." That was Tom Davisson and his use of the name sounded queer in that tense room. He seemed to have forgotten the rest of us were there and he was leaning forward with his hands gripping his knees and his voice was strange and strained. "You don't know what you're doing, Lucius. You've got to stay and see this through. You'd be right most any other time. But this time you're so damned wrong you could blow this town wide open."

"Why?" Judge Webb's voice had a sudden snap. "What makes this different?"

Tom looked at him and Tom's head came up higher and he seemed to be hunting for the right words. But he didn't have a chance to speak because Race Crim's voice cut in, a soft bitter voice coming from that flat expressionless face. "It's no use, Tom. His honor here has a record too he doesn't want busted."

Judge Webb's eyes flicked from Tom to Race and back and he pulled in his lips and blew them out again slow and gentle. He leaned forward, squeaking the swivel chair. "Tom. I appreciate your problem. You do not want to sit on the lid here with those two men till I can come back in a week or ten days. That is the best I can do and even that will take some date-juggling. I would like to stay and see this through but I have commitments that cannot be postponed. I should leave by early evening. But I will stretch it as far as I can for you. If these two men will plead guilty so I can dispense with a jury I will impress a lawyer for them and hurry it to a sentencing, if it keeps me over till late tonight."

Judge Webb leaned further forward to get his weight balanced and stood up and smoothed the front of his frock coat. Steady and deliberate he moved toward the inner door and Doc Schlegel stepped aside and he led the way back to the row of barred cells that crossed the rear room and we all followed. Tom stepped forward to unlock the cell doors and Judge Webb waved him back. The clerk stepped forward with his satchel and Judge Webb waved him back too. "We will require no accurate transcript of these proceedings," he said. He took his stand close to and midway between the cells occupied by Slater and the other prisoner. He studied them a moment, each in turn, and they stared back at him, Slater rising in the bunk to lean on one elbow and the other standing and shuffling his feet and moving away still facing out till he was against the rear wall.

"Gentlemen," Judge Webb said, "this is irregular but it is within the spirit of my official instructions. My commission empowers me to constitute my territorial court in whatever quarters seem to me proper and in accord with pressing circumstances. For the purposes of a preliminary hearing I declare this room my courtroom. Before any charge is cited against you it is my duty to inquire whether you wish the services of a lawyer at this hearing."

The other man shuffled his feet and tried to shrink further back and looked at Slater through the intervening bars. And Slater pushed himself up more and managed to swing both his legs over the edge of the bunk. "Preliminary only, eh, judge?" he said. "Just calling out charges? That it?"

"That is right," Judge Webb said.

Slater looked around at all the rest of us and his lips pulled in what might have been a strange grin or a soundless snarl or a combination of both. "No lawyer," he said.

"Good," Judge Webb said. "Mister Davisson, what is the first and foremost of the charges you wish to prefer against these men?"

"Murder," Tom said, short and quick.

"Mister Davisson," Judge Webb said, "be more specific."

"Planned murder," Tom said. "Committed during an assault on the United States mails on Tuesday the twenty-eighth of last month."

"That could be more officially phrased," Judge Webb said. "But it will suffice for the present. Gentlemen, I must inform you that if you plead guilty, in effect throw yourself upon the mercy of the court, your sentencing, after the evidence is presented, will lie wholly within the discretion of the presiding justice as limited by the pertinent statutes. In brief, myself. If you plead not guilty and a conviction follows, the direct recommendation of the jury will be immediate and binding. How do you plead?"

The question hung there in the air emphasizing the silence and all of us, Judge Webb too, looked only at Slater. The other man didn't count. It was Slater who was the focal point now as he had been from the beginning, an insignificant figure of meager flesh and bone made monstrous by the evil he had unleashed and that had enmeshed him too and yet of which at this instant because his was the decision he was still the dominant force. He looked around at us and you could see him almost tasting the situation and drawing some high excitement out of it and his lips pulled back further in that strange grin or snarl that was something beyond both. "Not guilty," he said.

We knew he would say it. We had known when we followed the judge through the inner doorway. We knew that Slater—and even though we didn't know anything about him really, not as a man that is, but only as a shadowy something that had a man's form and was behind the whole bitter business—we knew that he would play it out to the last possible push of circumstance. And yet we had followed and been bound up in the inevitable onward march of Judge Webb's words and had hung hopeful on the final waiting instant, waiting for Slater to speak. And he spoke and what we knew would happen had happened and the breath being released of each of us was clear in the quiet and Judge Webb's voice came, dry and matter-of-fact. "Very well. I bind you over for trial at the next term of my court in Goshen."

Somehow we were again in Tom's office. Not all of us. Not Race Crim. He was gone. It seemed to me I saw the outer door closing as I followed the others in. He must have gone then. And Doc Schlegel called his name and hurried to the door and was gone too. Meanwhile Judge Webb and his clerk took their same places and Tom took the same chair, slumping into it grim and tired and shoving his hands deep in his pants pockets. I took the wall and Luke Bowen stood by the door fidgeting his feet.

"What is bothering you, Mister Bowen?" Judge Webb said and Bowen grunted the words, "That damned gold."—"Sign a release and take it," Tom said. "Or leave it here. What the hell's the difference?"—"You keep it," Bowen said.

"When we're ready to ship again I'll let you know." He slipped out the door like he was glad to get away.

Judge Webb swung the swivel chair toward his clerk. "Write out what happened. Not the way it did. The way it should have. Make it legal and watertight. We don't want anyone picking holes in this case when we do get them to trial." He swung toward Tom. "You're getting old, Tom. All you have to do is hold them for a week. I promise to make it by then. And I will unlimber a speech in court this afternoon and send the people home. There will be no trouble. Only a few hotheads up this way. Why, I have seen you handle really ugly crowds and think that all in the day's work."

"I can do it," Tom said. "I can do it. This time I don't want to."

Judge Webb studied his plump fingers. "Personal feelings can be hard to live with," he said slow and gentle. "It's your job, Tom." He pressed his fingertips together and looked up to watch Tom and Tom said nothing, but Judge Webb must have seen something in Tom's face that satisfied him because he rocked up on his feet and his voice jumped to its usual rich roll. "Lock up and have lunch with me at the hotel. It will be time then to open court."

"No!" The word came out of Tom so sharp and sudden he seemed startled himself. "You made up your docket without me. Finish it the same. Take Burnett. He can act for me." Judge Webb pondered that and seemed to see sense in it and went straight out without saying anything more and I heard him calling around the side of the building to Dodd Burnett. His clerk scooped up the papers on the little table and swept them into his satchel and went out, quick and silent as he always was, and Tom and I were left alone.

Tom pulled his hands out of his pockets and turned them palms up and stared at them. Something under one fingernail bothered him and he picked at it till he had it out. He fished the makings out of his pockets and rolled a cigarette and lit it and took a long drag and dropped it on the floor and ground it out under a heel and stared at the tobacco shreds. I was uncomfortable against the wall and I went over to the chair the clerk had been using and straddled it so I was looking at Tom over the back of it with my chin resting on the top piece of wood. I felt empty and useless and then I realized I wasn't useless. I was somebody for him to talk to.

"Jess," he said, "do you know what went through my mind when he said 'not guilty'?"

"No," I said.

"I was thinking I ought to rig a way to have those two make a break so Race could cut them down."

"Why don't you?" I said.

He looked at me then, hard. "You know damn well why." He stood up and walked over and stared out the front window. "Maybe you don't know." He picked up the saddlebags and took them to the safe in the right back corner and opened it and put them in and closed and locked it. "Because that's the way I am. Right or wrong, that's it." He spun on a heel and went through the inner doorway and I heard him routing around in the storage room that opened off the big room where the cells were. He came back and he was carrying an old Army cot folded up. He unfolded it and pushed the little table aside and set the cot against the wall. "So you're not working for Bowen," he said. "So you're working for me."

"Doing what?" I said.

"Bringing me meals," he said. "And anything else I say. I'm not leaving this place till Rafferty can get here to spell me in shifts. Get word to him to leave somebody in charge at Stillwater and start at once. And bring some food. I'm damn hungry."

I stopped by the door. "How about those two back there?"

"Let them starve," he said. "That's Burnett's worry. If they don't eat till tonight they don't eat till tonight."

I went out and there was no one in front of the building but when I reached the main street there seemed to be more people than ever crowding the sidewalks, not moving much, just buzzing in bunches, and there was quite a collection far down the street by the hotel. I pushed along and no one paid much attention to me. They all seemed to know what had happened and I could catch chunks of talk as I went along. I reached the station and went in and to the agent and gave him the message for Rafferty. When he had the telegraph key chattering I went out and on to the squat two-story building with the false front that made it look like a three-story that was our hotel. I pushed in and to the left in the restaurant room where all four tables were in use I saw the three of them at one of the tables, Judge Webb eating calm and steady like he was home in his own quarters and Dodd

Burnett red-faced and self-important to be sitting there with
him and the clerk busy writing and reaching for a bite now
and then and writing again. Judge Webb saw me and his
head inclined just a bit and I felt like spitting in his eye. I
went straight through to the kitchen and told the woman
there what I wanted and she fussed around and fixed me a
basket with a clean dish towel over it. I went out and pushed
through the people up the street and around to Tom's office.
He was stretched on the cot staring at the ceiling. He sat
up and swung his legs over the side and I sat on the cot too
and began taking things out of the basket. He chewed awhile.

"See Race?" he said.—"No," I said.—"Good," he said.
"Hope Race is getting some rest." We both chewed awhile.
"Schlegel's right," I said. "They're talking most about that
drummer."—"Sure," he said. "That's natural."—"Not to
me," I said. "They didn't even know him."—"It was Billy's
job," he said. "Billy was paid to take risks. The drummer was just along for the ride. Like any of them might
be any time."—"Maybe so," I said. "But it ain't fair."—
"What's fair got to do with it?" he said. "It's the way things
are."

We chewed a while more and passed the coffee pitcher
back and forth. "You really going to squat here," I said, "till
the trial?"—"No," he said. "That's dumb heroics. Just till
I'm sure things are quiet. But I want Rafferty here so one
of us can be close by most of the time. Should have a guard.
Nighttime anyway."—"What if there's trouble outside?" I
said. "Somewhere around town."—"If there's trouble," he
said, "it'll be right here." We chewed and the coffee was
cooling so you could gulp it easy. "Been thinking over people
for deputies," he said. "Always end up with Rafferty. John's
a good man." We chewed some more and he shot a look at
me. "Thought of you, Jess," he said.—"No," I said. "I'm
staying out of this. I'm just running errands." He nodded
and we finished the food and I shoved the basket out of the
way with my foot. "Matter of fact," I said, "I'd be as far
away from this now as I could get wasn't for having to be
a witness at your damn trial." He nodded again and nudged
me off the cot and when I stood up he stretched out again.
"Go get some rest, Jess. We're all getting so wound up tight
without sleep we'll begin seeing things crooked. Appreciate
it if you bring me something soon after six."

I went out and toward the main street and I knew he

was right. I ought to try to get some sleep so maybe my mind would stop fighting and going on and on over all the arguments I'd been hearing and always coming back to the notion the way things had worked out wasn't fair to anybody except Slater and he was the one didn't deserve that. But I didn't turn left toward the Hatt House where my room was. I turned right and up the street to Bentley's Harness Shop. Mary Ella was there alone. I mean her father wasn't with her. Another man was, talking about buying a saddle and she was showing him several. I waited and she got brusque with him and he got a bit huffy and said he'd think about it and went out taking long steps and she almost hit me with the look she gave me.

"Jess," she said. "Jess Harker. You worry me all the time. You go off places where you might get shot again and you don't even come tell me you're safe when you get back. You let me find out things for myself. For all I know you might—"

"You don't really worry about me," I said. "You know me, I'm just a hop-skip-and-jump guy a girl can't depend—"

"Stop, Jess," she said. "Don't throw that up at me. I said it and I meant it but not the way you mean. I only want to—"

"You want," I said. "It don't make a—"

"Doesn't make," she said.

"It don't make," I said, "don't make, don't make, a damn bit of difference what you want me to do. You're like everybody else. Wanting me to do what maybe I don't want to do and be something I'm not. But there's one person around these parts takes me the way I am and don't—doesn't always keep trying to change me."

"You mean Race Crim," she said. "You think about him too much, Jess. You let him influence you too much."

"And why shouldn't I?" I said. "People say things about him and maybe he talks too much and likes to drink and isn't just the kind for a big job like with the Company but there isn't anybody ever knew him isn't proud to be his friend and anybody gets in a tough spot they'd rather have him there with them than anybody else that ever lived. And it isn't fair he's the one really getting kicked around most in this whole Slater business that wasn't really his fault only a little and he's more than made up for it."

I stopped talking. I hadn't meant to get started like that

anyway and now Calvin Bentley was standing in the doorway watching us. He came on in. "Jess," he said. "That was
a most interesting statement. I have heard the stories about
town and know perhaps all the pertinent facts. You suggest
much more meaning behind them. If you would talk, my
daughter and I would listen."

I wanted to talk. I hadn't any idea how much I wanted
to talk. Words were piling on top of each other in me and
even if she wouldn't marry me this was Mary Ella and her
father. I told them the whole story. I told them everything
they wouldn't have heard already about the doings at Big
Creek and then I told them about chasing Slater and at last
getting him. They listened and the only time one of them
said anything was when I told about Race shooting Slater
in the leg. Mary Ella reached out and put her hand on my
arm. "Race did that?" she said. "I didn't know he could be
like that." And I was grateful because she was showing me
she knew at least a little of how I felt and for a moment I
saw something plain. I saw that Race had one thing nobody
could ever take away from him. He was big. Tom Davisson
was the strongest and steadiest man likely I'd ever know.
But Race was the biggest. And then I told them what happened at Tom's office and when I finished I was more mixed
than I had been before.

"Mister Bentley," I said. "You're older than me. You
know plenty more. How can things be like that? So right
and wrong at the same time?"

"Jess," he said, "men have been asking that question
since there's any record of their thoughts. But I fail to follow
you. How do you apply it here?"

"Look, Mister Bentley," I said. "When you study it over,
Race's way is right. In this kind of country anyway. He's
quick and thorough. He's killed a lot of men at one time and
another but not a one that didn't deserve it and he was
certain when he did it. I know he shot Gene Gamble but
nobody'll ever make me think he didn't just wing Gamble
because he wasn't certain. But when you study it over too,
Tom's way is right. He wants the law to do it and be quick
and thorough too. But when Judge Webb gets to talking he
seems to be right too. How can they all be right and when
their ways get mixed together things be so wrong?"

"It could be," Calvin Bentley said, speaking slow and
like he wasn't just talking to a young one who might be

wanting to marry his daughter but to someone he could reason things out with that trouble a man. "It could be that the time for Race's way to be right in this territory is about over and what we need is Tom Davisson's way, or the judge's, which is the same only more so. But why do you keep saying the situation is working out wrong?"

"I don't know exactly," I said. "But Race won't be settled in his mind till those two men are dead, which they ought to be. But they won't be now. Not for a while. That isn't fair to him."

"Perhaps not to him," Calvin Bentley said. "Not in the immediate view. But to all the rest of us, yes. Judge Webb is trying to set a precedent for the benefit of all of us. It could even be for Race Crim sometime in the future. I would not worry, Jess. Another week and this will be over and everyone will be satisfied. A week of simmering down never hurt anyone." And that made sense but I kept having the feeling that making sense didn't really have much to do with the things that happened to people. But there wasn't anything to do. I was out of it. I was staying out of it now. Maybe I had been in it too much, thinking about it too much, and that was what was the matter with me. That and needing sleep.

When I went down the street to the Hatt House I had the plank sidewalk to myself. The people who had been there before must have crowded into our courtroom to see what might happen and hear what Judge Webb might have to say. The big downstairs barroom was empty except for Frank Hatt's bartender who was dunking glasses in a bucket and wiping them clean with a towel. I went straight through to the stairs at the rear and up and started along the hall to my room near the front. But I didn't get there. Not then. I stopped by the first door on the left and listened. That was Race's room, where he stayed when he was in town overnight. I thought I could hear breathing. I took hold of the door handle and turned it slow and pushed the door in enough for my head to peer around it. He was there, stretched out on the bed with his boots on and only his guns off. The two gunbelts were hanging from the footposts on the old brass bedstead. I thought he was asleep for a few seconds, then I knew he wasn't. I couldn't explain how I knew because his head was turned away from me toward the window. But

I knew his eyes were open and he was staring out at the dusty flat roof of the building next door. And then he startled me. Without turning his head to look at me and see who I was or even whether I was there, he spoke to me. He must have heard my steps and known them.

"Hello, kid," he said. "Come in. Or stay out. Or beat your brains against a brick wall. What the hell? It's all the same."

"Race," I said, moving in just enough to clear the door. "What'd you mean when you said the judge had a record to keep too? He isn't thinking just about himself. Maybe, the way things are nowadays, he's right."

Race didn't even hear. Or he didn't give any sign he did. He went on talking, as much to himself as me. "Go to sleep the doc tells me. Nice little man, the doc. Always liked him. But he doesn't know. That'll fix me up fine. So he says. He even finds his bag and gives me a shot of something. That'll do it he says. And it doesn't do a damn thing. Nothing will. Nothing'll stop me thinking." Race sat up and hitched himself in the bed till he was leaning against the brass rods of the headpiece. "Jess, what do you know about courts?"

"Not much," I said.

"You'll find out," he said. "They can smell and it ain't pretty. They can louse up things that are so damn simple so that after a while when the lawyers get wigging you can't tell hell from breakfast. Do you see it starting about those two bastards? We've got to have a nice proper trial and that takes time so there's delay. A week, two weeks, anything can happen, maybe a month or more. The judge gets persnickety and takes the case somewhere else. A clever lawyer gets his claws in and there's more postponements. Maybe a trial gets started and a juror lets slip he has his mind made up and whoop there's a mistrial and they have to start all over again. Maybe the bastards get hung and maybe they don't. Who's to say the jury won't get to thinking they're not so bad after all, they were hard up and didn't mean to play so rough so why not just salt them away in prison for a stretch."

"No jury'd do that," I said. "They're killers. Deliberate ones."

"No?" Race said. "There've been cases. And when you lock a man in prison that don't mean he'll stay there. There's always the chance he'll crack out or some friends'll take him or some soft-headed politician looking for votes'll wangle a pardon."

"Not those men," I said. "I don't believe it."

"You're so damn young," Race said. "How do we know this Slater hasn't some pretty strong friends down in the settlements? Give them time to get working and they can foul things up plenty. If people around here had the right kind of guts they'd grab him and the other one and swing them quick."

"No," I said. "They couldn't. Tom's watching. He's staying at the jail till Rafferty can get here. Then they'll take turns."

"He would," Race said. His voice was bitter. Suddenly he grinned at me and it was a strange kind of grin that made me feel uneasy. "Jess, how do you feel about this?"

"I'm not saying," I said. "I'm trying not to feel about it at all. I'm out and I'm staying out and I wish the whole damned thing never got started." Then I thought of something and maybe it was silly but it didn't seem so right then. "Race," I said. "Tom's been trying to think of deputies. But he can't. Not around here. That's why he's sending all the way for Rafferty. He'd be too proud to ask you. Why don't you go help him?"

The strangest look came over Race's face and he stared at me and he threw his head back so hard it hit against the brass bedstead and he began to laugh. "Me?" he managed to say. "Me help guard them?" He laughed till I was scared because it wasn't just an amused and funny-feeling laugh. It was too high-pitched and it had an edge that rasped my nerves. "Jess," he said, "appreciate me, don't you, kid?" Then he was as serious as before he had been laughing. "Don't do it, Jess. Don't keep building me up so damn much. Let me alone. You're doing right to stay out of it." He slid down full length on the bed again. "Get some sleep, Jess. Maybe I can too. You're better'n the doc. Maybe that joke was what I needed." He rolled his head to stare out the window again and there wasn't anything for me to do except go out and close the door and find my own bed and flop on it.

My room was on the same side and with my head turned on the pillow I could see the same dusty flat roof. I lay quiet thinking of myself lying there and Race down the hall on his bed and Tom on the cot at his office and Slater on the bunk in his cell, all of us lying quiet, each of us in a different place, yet all of us somehow bound together if only by our own thoughts. And it seemed to me as we lay quiet, the four of us, while almost everybody else in town was crowded into the courtroom where Judge Webb was driving forward in his deliberate and delaying way, we were all waiting for something, I didn't know what and I didn't want to try to think what. So I told myself that wanting to be out of it was not enough. I had to find some way to really be out of it. I thought I would ask Tom could I write out a statement of what I knew about the holdup, all the facts they might want from me, and swear to it for him and be free to go away like I'd been planning for so long. Then I'd be able to look back and see it plain and have time to work out in my mind what was right and what was wrong about the things I'd done and the others had done and maybe make sense out of the crazy-seeming pattern of living. That must have eased me because I dropped off into sleep and the last I was thinking was that I shouldn't sleep too long because Tom would be waiting for me around six.

I woke with a little jumping all over me and was on my feet before I remembered where I was. There was no sun through the window and the shadows outside were long. I was late already. And those few hours of rest hadn't done me much good. I felt more tired than before I lay down. I went into the hall and to the window at the front end that gave on to the street. Most of the wagons and buggies were gone. Only a few horses were left at the tie-rails. The sidewalks were about deserted. The few people there were regulars I recognized at once meandering along the way they always did. By pushing my cheek against the glass at the right side of the window I could see down the street and Luke Bowen was angling across toward the house where his wife would have supper waiting for him. He saw someone farther down, out of my range, maybe by the hotel, and waved an arm, easy and casual. The way he moved and the whole usual look of him told me that nothing had happened and nothing was going to happen. The relief I felt made me realize how worried I'd been. But it was plain now that Judge Webb had been right. The speech he'd promised to make must have sent people home. Goshen was like it always was, quiet and dusty and sort of drowsy for evening.

The sound of voices came faint from the barroom below and I turned and went along the hall and down the stairs. Frank Hatt was behind the bar and seven or eight men were bunched along it. I knew them all. Most of them were men you could find there any evening. A couple were from a piece out but they always took their drinks from Frank when they were in town. And Bert Foley was there but he would be too. He would have come to Goshen to be on hand as a witness if he'd been needed and he certainly would be taking on a drink or two before starting the long ride back to Big Creek. And what made the scene by the bar seem so natural was the man in the middle, the one holding the group together by his just being there like he always did—Race Crim, tall and handsome and looking like he'd never needed sleep in his life. The flush up his cheeks showed he had been drinking. He could drink steady as long as he wanted and the liquor never really got to him, just sent that flush up his cheeks and brightened his eyes. That was how he looked now, alive and alert with the vitality pumping through him and the pleasure of being alive and being Race Crim plain in every inch of him. That was how he used to be and seeing him like that again made me forget I'd ever been tired too.

The talking stopped and the room was hushed with everyone watching me when I reached the bottom of the stairs. That was natural too because Race was the only one knew I was upstairs that time of day. Bert Foley called to me and started over but Race took him by the arm.

"Hello, Jess," Race said. "Have a good sleep?"

"Must have," I said, "because I sure feel good now."

Nobody else said anything. Race was taking the lead and that was all right with me. The others didn't amount to much when he was around. "Going to see Mary Ella this evening, Jess?" he said.

"Why, yes," I said. "I expect so."

"Good idea," he said. "Stick with her, Jess. Stick with her." I thought he was thinking about things not being so good between her and me lately and meant I should keep trying, so I grinned and said I would and I wanted to stay and have a drink with him but I had a job to do first. I went out to the street and to the hotel and had an argument with the woman about not bringing back her basket but she fixed me another and I took it to Tom.

He was up and in his swivel chair listening to Dodd

Burnett report on the doings at court. He still looked tired
and the hair he had left was sticking out like rooster feathers
from his napping on the cot. "That's enough, Dodd," he said
when he saw me. "You've done so well maybe you can spell
me often in court when I feel lazy. But our guests back there
must be gnawing the bars by now. Haven't had a thing to
eat all day." Burnett stacked his papers neat and put them
on the desk and went through the inner doorway and began
rattling tin back where he kept cheap canned stuff to be
warmed on a kerosene burner. Tom went to a little mirror
hanging on the wall and began smoothing his hair. I started
unpacking the basket and putting the things on his desk. I'd
brought just enough for him, figuring to see if Mary Ella
would feed me. The atmosphere in that room was so easy
and normal that it was silly of me to jump so when someone
knocked on the door.

"Sit tight, Jess," Tom said and went to the door and
opened it a few inches. He opened it wider and stepped out
and closed it behind him and just as he closed it I had a
glimpse of Bert Foley outside. Tom stepped back in and
closed the door again and he wasn't the same man who had
gone out. The tiredness had dropped away from him. He
was straighter and bigger all over and his eyes were shining
in that hard face like he had been having a few drinks too.

"Jess," he said. "I knew it. I knew he wouldn't let me
down."

"Who?"

"Why, Judge Webb," Tom said. "He wants to see me
over at the hotel. A dollar'll get you a dozen he's changed
his mind and is staying over." Tom grabbed his hat out of
the corner and slapped dust out of it against his leg and
jammed it at an angle on his head. He was feeling good and
I was feeling the same right with him. "Keep an eye on
things here, Jess," he said, "till I get back. Won't take but
a minute or two." He went out the door bouncing off his
toes and closing it with a cheery slam behind him.

I finished unpacking the basket and the coffee smelled
tasty. I was lifting the pitcher to my lips when the thought
hit me, hard and low in the stomach, and my hand shook so
that some of the coffee spilled. Bert Foley hadn't been at
the hotel. He'd been at the Hatt House.

I put the pitcher down very careful. I didn't spill another
drop. The room was cold and empty and the silence in there

with me was so heavy I could feel it on my skin. I heard a
sound in the back room and remembered Dodd Burnett and
I could move. I went to the front window and stood against
the wall beside it and bent my neck so I could peer out. The
shadows had gone clear across the road by now and merged
into the general over-all shadow that was the beginning of
dusk. The deep shadow of the office where I was made me
feel a little safer. I studied the space outside and no one was
there, not anywhere my eyes could range. I was being silly.
Bert Foley could have gone to the hotel after I left the Hatt
House. The thing for me to do was to light the lamp and
drive the darkening chill out of the office and in a short while
Tom would be back and better than ever. And then I saw
them, the first of them, two figures where none had been
before, in the yard of the place across the road, in the dark
of the tree shadows there. I flattened more against the wall
and reached out along it to the door and pushed the bolt
into its socket.

"Dodd," I called, trying to make my voice carry without
being loud. He came hurrying in.

"Hey, why don't you light—"

"Shut up," I said, having trouble to keep my voice low
and not cracking. He froze and I could barely see his face
in the dying grayness of the room.

"Where's Tom?" he whispered.

"Gone," I said. "They got him away. Look here." He
came near me and peered around the window edge where
I pointed. There were five of them now, dark figures appearing from nowhere, maybe slipping up by separate ways.

"Let's get out of here," Dodd said.

"How?"

"A little window in the storage room. The grille opens
in." He didn't wait to see would I follow. He was gone,
tiptoeing in a frantic kind of running walk. I stayed flat
against the wall and tried to think and my mind wouldn't
go anywhere except to that window in the storage room. I
tried to straighten and my jacket bumped against the wall
with a small thud and my hand went into the right side
pocket. Billy Skinner's gun was there. And something else.
A deputy's badge. I had forgotten to give it back to Tom.
My hand closed over it and the points pressed into my fingers
and I squeezed harder because the sharp pain wasn't really
a pain but a shock that started my mind moving. I could see

it all now and I knew what would be out there and I looked again and I was right. I could make out seven figures and one of them was taller than the others and the outline of him was unmistakable. And the brutal cold of utter loneliness took me because those two murderers were behind me in Tom's jail and Race Crim was out there and he would be coming for them and I was between and there was no one else to do it. "God damn it," I was saying to myself over and over, unable to stop, and then I had to bite on my tongue to stop because they were moving and starting toward me. I pulled Billy Skinner's gun out of my pocket and I kneeled by the window and with the barrel of the gun I knocked the glass out of a corner and the tinkle of the breaking halted them across the road.

"Stop!" I shouted. "The door's locked and I've got a gun. You stay over there."

"Burnett?" someone called and Race's voice cut in. "That's not Burnett."

"You're damn right," I shouted. "Nobody's getting in here 'less Tom says so."

"Why, it's Jess," Race said and I could hear the relief in his tone. "It's the kid. This is me, Jess. Race. I'm taking over. Just unlock that door and skip. You'll be out of it."

But I couldn't be out of it. No matter how much I tried, I couldn't. I'd been in it from the beginning and I'd be in it till the end because somehow it wouldn't ever let me go. I was caught there and I was the only one at the moment and in that place who could do what had to be done and I was caught because that was the hard way things happen.

"No," I said. I wanted to say more but there were no words that could say what I wanted. That one word said it all. And Race's voice, confident and ringing with that vitality that could make him so magnificent, came at me.

"Stand aside, Jess. I'm coming. You'll not shoot me. Not me, boy." And he came running, head high and shoulders swinging, out of the darker shadows into the road toward me. I steadied the gun on the window sill and I blinked fast to keep the tears from blurring my eyes and I remembered something and deflected the barrel down till it was bearing on his legs driving toward me and I squeezed the trigger. And as I squeezed he tripped in a road rut and fell forward and what I saw down the sights in the instant of the gun's blast was the solid mass of his head against the broad shoulders hurtling into the terrible impact.

I heard afterwards that a lot happened during the next few minutes outside. The other men gathered around Race's body and argued back and forth some and one of them got a little crazy and pulled his gun and started blazing into the office. And Tom Davisson came leaping out of somewhere with his own gun blasting and dropped that one with a bullet through the right shoulder and stood and looked at Race and started cursing like no one had ever known him to do before and shouting at the rest of them to grab their guns so he'd have an excuse to drop them all. They faded away, glad to go. Even the one he'd hit got away by himself. And Tom was alone out there with Race and nobody'll ever know what he did then.

I expect I heard the shots and shouting but they didn't register on me. I was slumped on the floor by the window fighting the sobs that sought to wrench me apart and it was a long while before I had them licked and could lean my shoulders against the wall in a sort of numb stillness. The first I was really aware was when Tom lit the lamp and the light made me blink. He had brought Race's body in, smashing the lock with his shoulder, and laid it on the cot. I knew it was there without looking at it. I couldn't have done that. Tom stood looking down at me and he was older than I remembered him. And smaller. He was an old man, hard and gnarled like a piece of old rock, and his eyes were two small flat stones. It didn't seem particular important to me one way or another, but I told him anyway. "He wouldn't stop. I aimed for his legs. He stumbled."

Tom just looked at me and after a while he nodded as if what I said had got through to him. He seemed to change a little then and his eyes were different but I might have been imagining that. And after another while he spoke. "It should have been me," he said.

"No. It had to be me. He thought I'd be easy. He thought I wouldn't do it." And then I realized I hated Race. Dead or alive, I hated him. And I hated Tom Davisson. I hated the very guts of him standing there and looking at me. I hated everybody in the whole damned senseless world. All I wanted was to get away where everything would be new and I wouldn't know anybody and nobody would know me. And there he stood still holding strings on me.

"I suppose," I said, "you and your stinking law'll have to hold me now."

He shook his head. "Why, no. There'll be no charges. You were acting for me."

"Like hell I was. Don't try to pull it off me like that. I did it."

"All right, Jess," he said. "But there'll be no charges. No need even for an inquest."

"I suppose," I said, "that fat bastard of a judge might even try to thank me." He kept looking at me and I could see I was hitting him and I liked that.

"Judge Webb?" he said. "Might be fool enough. I won't let him."

"Stop being so damn noble," I said. "Or if you've got to be, try figuring a way I don't have to stick around here for that damn trial."

He studied me a moment and seemed to make up his mind. "That's easy," he said. "Skip any time you've a mind to. The case'll stand without you."

That was all I wanted to hear. I took the badge out of my pocket. I thought of throwing it at him and telling him I wished I'd never seen it or him. But I couldn't quite do that. I went over and laid it on his desk and kept my head turned so I wouldn't see Race and went out the door feeling stiff all over like an old man. The streets were empty, what there was of them in that scrubby little town. Except for a few lights through windows you wouldn't have known anybody even lived there. The Hatt House was closed, much as it ever was closed. The full doors that fitted behind the swinging doors were pushed to and there was only one lamp lit, the one back by the stairs that burned all night. I went in and up the stairs and along the hall in the dark with my hands out to feel the walls. In my room I shucked my jacket and let it fall anywhere on the floor and stretched out on the bed with my face in the pillow and it couldn't have been more than a minute before I was asleep.

The first light was easing in the window when I woke and that was what I wanted. I unscrewed the brass top of the right-hand post at the foot of the bed and fished out my roll and screwed the top on again. I slipped into my jacket and out into the hall and down the stairs. Even the man who

cleaned the place every morning wasn't stirring yet. I went
down the street past the quiet station and the hotel to the
livery stable and woke the night man and told him I wanted
to buy a horse. I didn't have much choice because he only
owned two. The others belonged to the boss who would be
sleeping at his place about a mile out of town. We reached
a price on the bigger of the two, a rangy dark bay, and I
paid the night man and yanked my bridle and saddle off their
peg on the wall and told him to slap them on. While he was
doing that I splashed some at the water trough and began
to be wide awake. I swung up and headed out the road to
the Gap. My plan was plain in my mind. I'd ride over to the
Gap and get the few things I had there and come back and
get the rest of my stuff and strike out from Goshen east
across the river at the one close ford and northeast then till
I hit the old Bozeman Trail and the fewer people I bumped
into till I was out of the territory the better. I'd been a
rolling stone and I hadn't gathered much moss. All I had
wouldn't make more than a good-sized saddle roll. But that
was all right. I was going to be rolling again.

A road runner jumped out the bushes flirting its tail
feathers and scooting ahead with tiny dust spurts and my
horse thought that a good idea and began stretching his own
legs. He was better than I had thought. He was soft and
would sweat too soon and too much but that would work out
of him in a few days. He had good action and he knew a
horse-man was talking to him along the reins, and the feel
of that leather in my hands was the nicest thing I could
remember for what seemed a long time. I slowed to save
the sweating and jogged along, taking the miles as they
came, and when the sun told me I might be meeting Uncle
Ben Nunan and young Wes Hatt on the coach I circled out
from the road a good distance and headed into the Gap from
the side.

I didn't spend any more time there than was necessary,
just enough to get my things and stop in the one general
store to have a few sandwiches made. The Gap wasn't much,
three houses, the store, a blacksmith shop and the barn used
for the coach and its old horses. There wasn't even a stock
tender. It was the driver's job to take care of the horses
there. I didn't see more than four people and they looked
at me curious but I didn't encourage any talking and pulled
out quick as I could. I wasn't sorry to see the last of that

place. I'd spent too many long hours worrying away the time there, waiting to make the return trip to Goshen, time I could have spent but didn't getting to know Uncle Ben better or reading some of the books Calvin Bentley would have let me take. I knew every rock and bush for miles around too damn well from long tramping around by myself killing the hours.

It was about half past noon when I was in sight of Goshen again. I'd been going slow. There wasn't any sense wearing my horse out the first day. He'd have more miles to go soon as I packed my moss. And I'd been off the road a few times, swinging out to avoid a wagon one time and a couple of riders another. I came into town from the right, away from the road, and to the livery stable from the rear. I told the day man to feed and water my horse and give him a good rubdown. I slipped out of the stable and behind the buildings to the back way into the Hatt House. And inside the lean-to shed, sitting on the steps that led into the building, was Uncle Ben Nunan.

"Figured you'd come this way," he said. "Jess, boy, it's not right to skip without saying a little something to your friends."

I looked at him sitting there, a small and shriveling old man with his not-so-old eyes shining, and I didn't hate him. I didn't hate anybody. I was just numb toward him and toward the whole world outside of myself. "All right," I said. "So I'll say something. Good-bye."

"Don't hurry, Jess," he said. "Bowen wants to see you."

"That's too damn bad," I said, "because I don't want to see him." I started to push past on the steps and Uncle Ben moved so I couldn't without stepping on him.

"Don't go up there yet," he said. "Have something to tell you. Bowen said I could. The Company's planning to shove the main line up to the gold creeks. Probably station at North Forks. Grading crew starts tomorrow topping off the worst humps. First coach to roll in about three weeks. A nice run, Jess. Fifty-odd miles that'll sweat it out of any driver and the best horses. Bowen thinks maybe you'd do."

I stumbled back and bumped against a barrel and grabbed hold of it because I was shaking. I wasn't numb anymore. I was so shaking mad I could have hoisted that barrel and thrown it at him. "God damn it," I said. "Bowen's crazy.

Everybody's crazy. I plug along on that crawling Gap run.
I take his coach through to Stillwater with a bullet hole in
me. I even go back to that lousy little run that a pink-fuzzed
boy like Wes Hatt can drive. And he keeps kicking me around
like a damned dog. Then I go kill a man and the best goddam
fool of a man anywhere around and right away he offers me
something like that."

Uncle Ben didn't pay any attention to my shouting. He
waited for me to finish. "Why, no," he said. "Not because
you killed Race. That was an accident. But because you did
something else at the same time. You've added considerable
age this past week. And when the chips were down you
showed where you stood." Uncle Ben pushed himself up with
his good arm and stood on the steps. "Take the job or don't
take the job. That's not so important, Jess." I couldn't speak
and he moved down and out of the way. "Go on upstairs,
Jess. Be as mad as you want. But the job'll be open till you
make up your mind." He moved past me and put a hand on
my shoulder as he went by and I was alone in the shed.

I leaned against the barrel till I wasn't shaking anymore,
not any part of me. When I went inside and close around
the doorway to the stairs the big barroom was empty except
for Frank Hatt on a chair by one of the wide front windows
reading a paper. He looked over it at me and his face was
kind of funny for a second or two because he had been one
of them and he knew I knew that. Then he grinned at me
kind of sheepish and jerked a hand with the thumb pointing
upstairs and went back to his paper. I walked along the
narrow hall and stopped by Race's door and opened it. The
room was bare. The old Company jacket with the torn sleeve
that'd been on a hook by the bed was gone. All of his things
were gone. *Yes*, I thought, *Tom's been here. It would have
to be done so he'd do it.* I closed the door after me and walked
along the hall to my room and opened the door and Mary
Ella was there. She was sitting on the one chair, her hands
folded in her lap and her head down. She raised her head
and saw me. "Jess," she said, "you took a long time."

I moved a little and gave the door a slight push and it
closed with a soft snap and I leaned against the wall beside
it. "Uncle Ben told me," she said. "Are you taking the job?"
I couldn't answer because I didn't know. She waited and her
head rose higher. "Then you're going away," she said. "This

time really." And her head rose higher till her chin was out firm and the clear line of her neck was taut as she looked up across the room at me. "I'm going with you."

I moved again and sank down on the edge of the bed because I was worried my knees would buckle. But I still couldn't speak. "Jess," she said, "don't you want to marry me?"

I looked at her and she wasn't just the girl I once thought I wanted walking fresh and feminine beside me where people could see, and eager and responding in my arms when we were alone. She was a safeness and a warm comfort. But I couldn't say that. "I don't know," I said. "I don't know anything anymore. I don't know what I'm going to do. Nothing makes sense. You wouldn't go with me when I was all right and knew what I wanted to do. Now you say you will when I don't really feel like wanting to do anything, just maybe getting away and trying to—"

"Jess," she said, "I wouldn't go with you before because you were just a foot-loose kid and I was afraid. That was a long time ago. I'm not afraid now. It doesn't matter what you do or where you go. I'm going. Because I'll be going with a man." She came over and sat beside me on the bed, not too close, just close enough so she could reach out a hand and I could take hold of it. "Jess, I was talking to Tom this morning."

"No," I said. "I don't want to hear about him. I don't want ever to see him again." But she went straight on. "He helped me to understand. He said you'd probably be going and perhaps it would be right for you to do that. But he said it didn't make any difference where or how far, he wouldn't have to worry about you any more."

"Tom said that?" It was funny but I could speak his name and think about him again. I could even see that in time I might be able to talk to him and be with him and watch his eyes maybe be different in the hard rock of his face. I felt old, not in years but in living and what life could do to me. *Maybe,* I thought, *maybe I've got my full growth at last.* Things were so much easier when I was young and living was simple and black was black and white was white without the endless shading gradations between and I was not even aware of the bitter choices that could be exacted by the passing days. *If this is being a man,* I thought, *I don't like it. But I can't change it.* Then I felt Mary Ella's hand tightening on mine and I realized she knew and it could be the same for her and that was better.

A whistle sounded outside, high and sweet, faint and half a block away. A voice drifted after, "Roll 'em." A whip cracked and hooves pounded in the clean swinging rhythm of a six-horse pull and the soft creakings of oiled leather floated in the dusty air over the street. The afternoon coach was starting its long run down the main line. We listened together till the sound of the hooves had faded and merged away into the rhythm of our own pulse beats. We sat side by side on the bed and looked out the window over the flat rooftop and on past the other buildings to the open stretches where the road to the Gap ran to the far horizon. We looked out together into the great ranging world where coach wheels were rolling out the miles and the only thing that made sense was loving someone and doing a job and taking what life gave without whimpering or running away.

JACOB

hose moccasins? Mine. Though I never wore them. Had them on just once to see if they fitted. They did. A bit tight but I could get them on.

Don't touch them. The leather's old and dry and the stitching rotted. Ought to be. They've been hanging there a long time. Look close and you can see the craftsmanship. The best. They're Nez Percé moccasins. Notice the design worked into the leather. It's faint now but you can make it out. Don't know how they did that but the Nez Percé could really work leather. A professor who studied such things told me once that design means they're for a chief. For his ceremonial appearances, sort of his dress-up footwear. Said only a chief could use that design. But it's there. Right there on those moccasins.

Yes. They're small. Boy size. That's because I was a boy then. But they're a chief's moccasins all the same. Kept them down the years because I'm proud of them. And because they mind me of a man. He had a red skin. Copper would be closer the color. A muddy copper. And I only saw him once. But he was a man.

* * *

That was a long way from here. A long way. In years and in miles. I was ten then, maybe eleven, maybe twelve, in that neighborhood, I disremember exactly. Best I can do is place it in the late seventies. Funny how definite things like dates and places slip away and other stray things, like the way you felt at certain times and how your first wild strawberries tasted, can remain clear and sharp in your mind. We were living, my folks and my older brother and myself, in a little town in eastern Montana. Not much of a place. Just a small settlement on the railroad that wouldn't have amounted to anything except that it had a stretch of double track where a train going one direction could pull off to let one going the other get past. My father was a switch-man. Looked after track and handled the west-end switch. That was why we were there.

The Indian smell was still in the air in those days. People around here and nowadays wouldn't know what that means. It was a knowing and a remembering that not so far away were still real live free-footed fighting Indians that might take to raiding again. They were pegged on treaty lands and supposed to stay there. But they were always hot over one thing or another, settlers gnawing into their hunting grounds or agents pinching their rations or maybe the government forgetting to keep up treaty payments. You never knew when they might get to figuring they'd been pushed far enough and would start council fires up in the hills and come sudden and silent out of the back trails, making trouble. It was only a year or two since the Custer affair on the Little Big Horn southwest of where we were. No-one with any experience in those things expected the treaty that ended that business to hold long.

Don't take me wrong. We didn't look for Indians behind bushes and sit around shivering at night worrying about attacks. The nearest reservation was a fair jump away and if trouble started we'd know about it long before it reached us, if it ever did. Matter of fact it never did. I grew up in that territory and never once was mixed in any Indian trouble past an argument over the price of a blanket. Never even saw any fighting Indians except this once I'm telling about and then they weren't fighting any more. It was just a smell in the air, the notion there might be trouble any time. Indians were quite a topic when I was a boy and the talk of an evening chewed it plenty.

Expect I heard as much of it as any of the boys around our settlement. Maybe more. My father had been in the midst of the Sioux outbreak in Minnesota in the early sixties. He'd seen things that could harden a man. They settled his mind on the subject. "Only good Indian," he'd say, "is a dead one." Yes. That's not just a saying out of the storybooks. There were men who really said it. And believed it. My father was one. Said it and believed it and said it so often I'd not be stretching the truth past shape to figure he averaged it couple times a week and so naturally we boys believed it too, hearing it all the time. I'll not argue with anyone wants to believe it even today. I'm only telling you what happened to me.

Hearing that kind of talk we boys around the settlement had our idea what Indians were like. I can speak for myself anyway. The Indians I saw sometimes passing through on a train or loafing around a town the few times I was in one with the folks didn't count. They were tame ones. They were scrawny mostly and they hung around where white people were and traded some and begged liquor when they couldn't buy it. They weren't dangerous or even interesting. They didn't matter more'n mules or dogs or anything like that cluttering the landscape. It was the wild ones filled my mind, the fighting kind that lived the way they always had and went on the warpath, and made the government send out troops and sign treaties with them. Can't recall exactly what I thought they looked like, but they were big and fierce and dangerous and they liked to burn out homesteaders' cabins and tie people to wagon wheels and roast them alive over slow fires, and it took a brave man to go hunting them and look at them down the sights of his gun. Days I felt full of ginger I'd plan to grow up quick and be an Indian fighter. Late afternoon, before evening chores, I'd scout the countryside with the stick I used for a gun and when I'd spot a spray of red sumac poking out of a brush clump, I'd belly-it in the grass and creep to good cover and poke my gun through and draw my bead. I'd pull on the twig knob that was my trigger and watch careful, and sometimes I'd have to fire again and then I'd sit up and cut another notch on the stick. I had my private name for that. Making good Indians, I called it.

What's that got to do with those moccasins? Not much I guess. But I'm telling this my way. It's all part of what I remember when I sit back and study those moccasins a spell.

The year I'm talking about was a quiet one with the Sioux but there was some Indian trouble all right, along in the fall and a ways away, over in the Nez Percé country in Idaho. It started simple enough like those things often did. There was this band lived in a valley, maybe seven hundred of them all told, counting the squaws and young ones. Biggest safe estimate I heard was three hundred braves, fighting men I mean. Can't remember the name of the valley, though I should. My brother settled there. But I can recall the name of the chief. That sticks. Always will. Not the Indian of it because that was a fancy mouthful. What it meant. Mountain Elk. Not that exactly. Big-Deer-That-Walks-the-High-Places. Mountain Elk is close enough. But people didn't call him that. Most Indians had a short name got tagged to them somehow and were called by it. His was Jacob. Sounded funny first time I heard it but not after I'd been hearing it a while.

As I say, this trouble started simple enough. We heard about it from the telegraph operator at the settlement who took his meals at our place. He picked up information relaying stuff through his key. News of all kinds and even military reports. Seems settlers began closing in around Jacob's valley and right soon began looking at the land there. Had water which was important in that country. Some of them pushed in and Jacob and his boys pushed them back out. So complaints were being made and more people wanted to move in, and talk went around that land like that was too good for Indians anyway because they didn't use it right, the way white men would, and when there was enough steam up a government man went in to see Jacob. Suggested the band would be better off living on some outside reservation. Get regular rations and have an agent to look after them. No, Jacob said, he and his were doing all right. Had been for quite a spell and expected to keep on doing the same. Sent his thanks to the Great White Chief for thinking about him but he wasn't needing any help. So after a while the presure was stronger and another government man went in. Offered to buy the land and move the band in style to a reservation. No, said Jacob, he and his children—he called them all his children though he wasn't much past thirty himself—he and his children liked their land and weren't interested in selling. Their fathers had given up land too much in the past and been forced to keep wandering and had found this place when no one wanted it, and it was good and they had stayed there. Most of them then living had been born there and they wanted to die there too and that was that.

Well, the pressure went on building and there were ruckuses here and yonder around the valley when some more settlers tried moving in and a bunch of young braves got out of hand and killed a few. So another government man went in, this time with a soldier escort. He didn't bother with arguing or bargaining. He told Jacob the Great White Chief had issued a decree and this was that the whole tribe was to be moved by such and such a date. If they went peaceable, transportation would be provided and good rations. If they kept on being stubborn, soldiers would come and make them move and that would be a bad business all around. Yes, said Jacob, that would be a bad business but it wouldn't be his doing. He and his children wouldn't have made the storm but they would stand up to it if it came. He had spoken and that was that.

So the days went along toward the date set which was in the fall I'm telling about. Jacob and his band hadn't made any preparations for leaving and the officer in charge of this whole operation thought Jacob was bluffing and he'd just call that bluff. He sent about four hundred soldiers under some colonel into the valley the week before the moving was supposed to happen, and Jacob and the others, the whole lot of them, just faded away from their village and off into the mountains behind the valley. The colonel sent scouting parties after them but couldn't make contact. He didn't know what to do in that situation so he set up camp there in the valley to wait and got real peeved when some of Jacob's Nez Percés slipped down out of the mountains one night and stampeded his stock. Finally he had his new orders and on the supposed moving day he carried them out. He put his men to destroying the village and they wiped it level to the ground, and the next morning early there was sharp fighting along his upper picket lines and he lost quite a few men before he could jump his troops into the field in decent force.

That was the beginning. The government wanted to open the valley for homesteading but couldn't without taking care of Jacob first. This colonel tried. He chased Jacob and his band into the mountains and thought overtaking them would be easy with the squaws and young ones slowing Jacob down, but Jacob had hidden them off somewhere and was traveling light with his braves. He led this colonel a fast run through rough country and caught him off watch a few times and whittled away at his troops every odd chance till this colonel had to turn back, not being outfitted for a real campaign. When he, that'd be this colonel, got back he found Jacob had beat him there and made things mighty unpleasant for those left holding the camp before slipping away again. About this time the government realized what it was up against and recalled the colonel and maybe whoever was his boss, and assigned a general—a brigadier—to the job and began mounting a real expedition.

We heard plenty about what happened after that, not just from the telegraph operator but from my brother who was busting the seams of his breeches those days and wanting to strike out for himself, and signed with the freighting company that got the contract carting supplies for the troops. He didn't see any of the fighting but he was close to it several times and he wrote home what was happening. Once a week he'd promised to write and did pretty well at it. He'd send his letters along to be posted whenever any of the wagons were heading back, and my mother would read them out to my father and me when they arrived. Remember best the fat one came after he reached the first camp and saw Jacob's valley. Took him two chunks of paper both sides to tell about it. Couldn't say enough about the thick green grass and the stream tumbling into a small lake and running quiet out again, and the good trees stepping up the far slopes and the mountains climbing on to the end of time all around. Made a man want to put his feet down firm on the ground and look out steady like the standing trees and stretch tall. Expect that's why my brother quit his job soon as the trouble was over and drove his own stakes there.

Yes. I know. I'm still a long way from those moccasins. I'm over in Idaho in Jacob's valley. But I get to remembering and then I get to forgetting maybe you're not interested in all the sidelines of what I started to tell you. I'll try to move it faster.

As I was saying, the government outfitted a real expedition to go after Jacob. A brigadier general and something like a thousand men. There's no point telling all that happened except that this expedition didn't accomplish much more than that first colonel and his men did. They chased Jacob farther and almost penned him a few times and killed a lot of braves and got wind of where his women and their kids were hidden, and forced him to move them farther into the mountains with them getting out just in time, not being able to carry much with them. But that wasn't catching Jacob and stopping him and his braves from carrying on their hop-skip-and-jump war against all whites in general and these troops in particular. Then a second general went in and about a thousand more soldiers with them and they had hard fighting off and on over a couple hundred miles and more, and the days drove on into deep winter and Jacob was licked. Not by the government and its soldiers and their guns. By the winter. He and his braves, what was left of them, had kept two generals and up to two thousand troops busy for four months fighting through parts of three states and then the winter licked him. He came to the second general under truce in what remained of his Chief's rig and took off his headdress and laid it on the ground and spoke. His children were scattered in the mountains, he said, and the cold bit sharp and they had few blankets and no food. Several of the small ones had been found frozen to death. From the moment the sun passed overhead that day he would fight no more. If he was given time to search for his children and bring them together he would lead them wherever the Great White Chief wished.

There. I'm closer to those moccasins now even though I'm still way over in Idaho. No. Think it was in western Montana where Jacob surrendered to that second general. Well, the government decided to ship these Nez Percés to the Dump, which was what people called the Indian Territory where they chucked all the tribes whose lands weren't just cut down but were taken away altogether. That meant Jacob and his children, all that was left of them, about three hundred counting the squaws and kids, would be loaded on a special train and sent along the railroad that ran through our settlement. These Nez Percé Indians would be passing within a stone's throw of our house and we would have a chance to see them at least through the windows and maybe, if there was need for switching, the train would stop and we would have a good look.

Wonder if you can scratch up any real notion what that meant to us boys around the settlement. To me maybe most of all. These weren't tame Indians. These were wild ones. Fighting Indians. About the fightingest Indians on record. Sure, the Sioux wiped out Custer. But there were a lot more Sioux than soldiers in that scuffle. These Nez Percés had held their own mighty well against a big chunk of the whole United States Army of those days. They were so outnumbered it had got past being even a joke. Any way you figured, it had been about one brave to six or seven soldiers and those braves hadn't been well armed at the start and had to pick up guns and ammunition as they went along from soldiers they killed. Some of them were still using arrows at the finish. I'm not being funny when I tell you they kept getting bigger and fiercer in my mind all the time I was hearing about that long running fight in the mountains. It was notches for Nez Percés I was cutting on my stick now and the way I felt about them, even doing that took nerve.

The day came the train was to pass through, some time late afternoon was the first report, and all of us settlement boys stayed near the telegraph shack waiting. It was cold, though there wasn't much snow around. We'd sneak into the shack where there was a stove, till the operator was peeved at our chattering and shooed us out, and I expect I did more than my share of the chattering because in a way these were my Indians because my brother was connected with the expedition that caught them. Don't think the other boys liked how I strutted about that. Well, anyway, the sun went down and we all had to scatter home for supper and the train hadn't come. Afterwards some of us slipped back to the shack and waited some more while the operator cussed at having to stick around waiting for word, and one by one we were yanked away when our fathers came looking for us, and still the train hadn't come.

It was some time past midnight and I'd finally got to sleep when I popped up in bed at a hammering on the door. I looked into the kitchen. Father was there in his nightshirt opening the outside door and the operator was on the step cussing some more that he'd had word the train was coming, would get there in half an hour, and they'd have to switch it and hold it till the westbound night freight went past. Father added his own cussing and pulled on his pants and boots and heavy jacket and lit his lantern. By the time he'd

done that I had my things on too. My mother was up then
and objecting, but my father thought some and shushed her.
"Fool kid," he said, "excited about Indians all the time. Do
him good to see what thieving smelly things they are." So
I went with him. The late moon was up and we could see
our way easy and I stayed in the shack with the operator
and my father went off to set his signal and tend his switch.
Certain enough, in about twenty minutes the train came
along and swung onto the second line of track and stopped.

The telegraph operator stepped out and started talking
to a brakeman. I was scared stiff. I stood in the shack doorway and looked at the train and I was shaking inside like I
had some kind of fever. It wasn't much of a train. Just an
engine and little fuel car and four old coaches. No caboose.
Most trains had cabooses in those days because they carried
a lot of brakemen. Had to have them to wrangle the hand
brakes. Expect the brakeman the operator was talking to
was the only one this train had. Expect that was why it was
so late. I mean the railroad wasn't wasting any good equip-
ment and any extra men on this train, and it was being
shoved along slow when and as how between other trains.

I stood there shaking inside and the engine was wheezing
some and the engineer and fireman were moving slow and
tired around it, fussing with an oilcan and a tin of grease.
That was the only sign of life I could see along the whole
train. What light there was in the coaches, only one lantern
lit in each, wasn't any stronger than the moonlight outside
and that made the windows blank-like and I couldn't see
through them. Except for the wheezing engine, that train
was a tired and sleeping or dead thing on the track. Then
I saw someone step down from the first coach and stretch
and move into the moonlight. He was a soldier, a captain,
and he looked tired and sleepy and disgusted with himself
and the whole world. He pulled a cigar from a pocket and
leaned against the side of the coach, lighting the cigar and
blowing out smoke in a slow puff. Seeing him so lazy and
casual, I stopped shaking and moved into the open and closer
to the coach and shifted around trying to find an angle that
would stop the light reflection on the windows and let me
see in. Then I stopped still. The captain was looking at me.
"Jee-sus," he said. "Why does everybody want to gawk at
them? Even kids." He took a long drag on his cigar and blew
a pair of fat smoke rings. "You must want to bad," he said.

"Up so late. Go on in, take a look." I stared at him, scared now two ways. I was scared to go in where those Indians were and scared not to, after he'd said I could and just about ordered I should. "Go ahead," he said. "They don't eat boys. Only girls. Only at lunchtime." And sudden I knew he was just making a tired joke, and it would be all right and I went up the steps to the front platform and peered in.

Indians. Fighting Indians. The fighting Nez Percés who had led United States soldiers a bloody chase through the mountains of three states. The big and fierce redmen who had fought many times their own number of better armed soldiers to a frequent standstill in the high passes. And they weren't big and they weren't fierce at all. They were huddled figures on the coach seats, two to a seat down the twin rows, braves and squaws and young ones alike, all dusty and tired and hunched together at the shoulders in drowsy silence or sprawled apart over the window sills and seat arms in sleep. In the dim light they looked exactly like the tame Indians I'd seen, and they seemed to shrink and shrivel even more as I looked at them and there was no room in me for any emotion but disappointment, and when I noticed the soldiers sleeping in the first seats close to me I sniffed to myself at the silly notion any guards might be needed on that train. There wasn't the slightest hint of danger anywhere around. Being on that train was no different from being off it except that it was being on a stopped train and not being outside on the ground. It didn't even take any particular nerve to do what I did when I started walking down the aisle.

The only way I know to describe it is that I was in a sort of trance of disappointment and I wanted to see everything and I went straight down the aisle looking all around me. And those Indians acted like I wasn't there at all. Those that were awake. Each of them had his eyes fixed somewhere, maybe out a window or at the floor or just at some point ahead, and didn't move them. They knew I was there. I could tell that. A feeling. A little crawling on my skin. But they wouldn't look at me. They were somehow off away in a place all their own and they weren't going to let me come near getting in there with them or let me know they even saw me outside of it. Except one. He was a young one, a boy like me only a couple of years younger, and he was scrooged down against a sleeping brave—maybe his father —and his small eyes, solid black in the dim light, looked at me, and his head turned slow to keep them on me as I went past and I could sense them on me as I went on till the back of the seat shut them off.

Still in that funny trance I went into the next coach and through it and to the third coach and on to the last. Each was the same. Soldiers slumped in sleep, and the huddled figures of the Indians in different pairings and sprawled positions but the effect the same and then at the end of the last car I saw him. He had a seat to himself and the headdress with its red-tipped feathers hung from the rack above the seat. He was asleep with an arm along the window sill, his head resting on it. I stopped and stared at him and the low light from the lantern near the end of the coach shone on the coppery texture of his face and the bare skin of his chest where it showed through the fallen-apart folds of the blanket wrapped around him. I stared at him and I felt cheated and empty inside. Even Jacob wasn't big or fierce. He wasn't as big as my father. He was short. Maybe broad and rather thick in the body but not much, even that way. And his face was quiet and—well, the only word I can ever think of is peaceful. I stared at him and then I started a little because he wasn't sleeping. One eyelid had twitched a bit. All at once I knew he was just pretending. He was pretending to be asleep so he wouldn't have to be so aware of the stares of anyone coming aboard to gawk at him. And sudden I felt ashamed and I hurried to the back platform to leave the train, and in the shadow there I stumbled over a sleeping soldier and heard him rousing himself as I scrambled down the steps.

That started what happened afterwards. Expect I'm really to blame for it all. Mean to say it probably wouldn't have happened if I hadn't been hurrying and wakened that soldier. He didn't know I was there. He was too full of sleep at first and didn't know what had awakened him. While I stayed in the dark shadow by the coach, afraid to go out into the moonlight, he stood up and stretched and came down the steps without noticing me and went around the end of the train toward the wider shadow on the other side, and as he went I saw him pulling a bottle out of a pocket. I felt safe again and started away and turned to look back, and the light was just right for me to see some movement inside through the window by the last seat. Jacob was standing up. All kinds of wild notions poured through my mind and

I couldn't move and then he was emerging through the rear door on to the platform and I wasn't exactly scared because I wasn't conscious of feeling anything at all except that I couldn't move. Time seemed to hang there motionless around me. Then I realized he wasn't doing anything and wasn't going to do anything. He wasn't even aware of me or if he was I was without meaning for him and he had seen me and dismissed me. He was standing quiet by the rear railing and his blanket was left inside and the cold night air was blowing against his bare chest above his leather breeches but he didn't appear to notice that. He was looking back along the double iron line of the track toward the tiny point of light that was my father's lantern by the west switch. He stood there, still and quiet, and I stayed where I was and watched him and he did not move and stood there looking far along the westward track and that was what we were doing, Jacob and I, when the soldier came back around the end of the train.

Thinking about it later I couldn't blame that soldier too much. Maybe had orders to keep the Indians in their seats or not let them on the rear platform or something like that. Probably was worried about drinking on duty and not wanting to be caught letting anything slip with the tang plain on his breath. Could be too he'd taken on more than he could handle right. Anyway he was surprised and mad when he saw Jacob standing there. He reached first and pulled some object off the platform floor and when he had it I could see it was his rifle. Then he jumped up the steps and started prodding Jacob with the rifle barrel toward the door. Jacob looked at him once and away and turned slow and started to move and the soldier must have thought Jacob moved too slow because he swung the gun around to use the stock end like a club and smack Jacob on the back. I couldn't see exactly what happened then because the scuffle was too sudden and quick but there was a blur of movement and the soldier came tumbling off the platform to the ground near me and the gun landed beside him. He was so mad he tripped all over himself getting to his feet and scrabbling for the gun and he whipped it up and hip-aimed it at Jacob and tried to fire it and the breech mechanism jammed some way and he clawed at it to make it work.

And Jacob stood there on the platform, still and quiet again, looking down at the soldier with bare breast broadside to the gun. I could see his eyes bright and black in the moonlight and the shining on the coppery firmness of his face and he did not move and of a sudden I realized he was waiting. He was waiting for the bullet. He was expecting it and waiting for it and he would not move. And I jumped forward and grabbed the rifle barrel and pulled hard on it. "No," I shouted. "Not like that." And the soldier stumbled and fell against me and both of us went down and someone was yelling at us and when I managed to get to my feet I saw it was the captain and the soldier was up too, standing stiff and awkward at attention. "Bloody Indian," the soldier said. "Trying to get away." The captain looked up and saw Jacob standing there and jerked a bit with recognizing who it was. "He was not," I said. "He was just standing there." The captain looked at the soldier and shook his head slow. "Jee-sus," he said. "You'd have shot that one." The captain shook his head again like he was disgusted and tired of everything and maybe even of living. "What's the use," he said. He flipped a thumb at the soldier. "Pick up your gun and get on forward." The soldier hurried off and the captain looked at Jacob and Jacob looked down at him, still and quiet and not moving a muscle. "There's fools of every color," the captain said and Jacob's eyes brightened a little as if he understood and I expect he did because I'd heard he could speak English when he wanted to. The captain wiped a hand across his face. "Stand on that damned platform as long as you want," he said. He remembered he had a cigar in his other hand and looked at it and it was out and he threw it on the ground and swung around and went toward the front of the train again, and I wanted to follow him but I couldn't because now Jacob was looking at me.

He looked down at me what seemed a long time and then he motioned at me and I could tell he wanted me to step out further into the moonlight. I did and he leaned forward to peer at me. He reached a hand out toward me, palm flat and down, and said something in his own language and for a moment I was there with him in the world that was different and beyond my own everyday world and then he swung away and stepped to stand by the rear railing again and I knew I was outside again, outside of his mind and put away and no more to him than any other object around. He was alone there looking far down the track and it sank slow and deep in me that he was looking far past the tiny light point of my father's lantern, far on where the lone track ran straight along the slow-rising reaches of distance into the horizon that led past the longest vision at last to the great climbing mountains. He was looking back along the iron trail that was taking him and his children away from a valley that would make a man want to put his feet firm on the earth and stretch tall and was taking them to an unknown place where they would not be themselves any longer but only some among many of many tribes and tongues and all dependent on the bounty of a forgetful government. It wasn't an Indian I was seeing there anymore. It was a man. It wasn't Jacob, the tamed chief that even foolish kids could gawk at. It was Mountain Elk, the Big-Deer-That-Walks-the-High-Places and he was big, really big, and he was one meant to walk the high places.

He stood there looking down the track and the westbound night freight came rumbling out of the east and strained past, and he stood there watching it go westward along the track and his train began to move, creeping eastward slow and feeling forward, and I watched it go and long as I could see him he was standing there, still and quiet, looking straight out along the back trail.

Well. I've taken you to where I was headed. It's only a hop now to those moccasins. I tried to tell the other boys about it the next day and likely boasted and strutted in the telling and they wouldn't believe me. Oh, they'd believe I saw the Indians all right. Had to. The telegraph operator backed my saying I was there. Even that I went aboard. But they wouldn't believe the rest. And because they wouldn't believe me I had to keep pounding it at them, telling it over and over. Expect I was getting to be mighty unpopular. But Jacob saved me even though I never saw him again. There was a day a bunch of us boys were playing some game or other back of the telegraph shack and sudden we realized someone had come up from somewhere and was watching us. An Indian. Seemed to be just an ordinary everyday sort of tame Indian. But he was looking us over intent and careful and he picked me and came straight to me. He put out a hand, palm flat and down, and said something to me in his Indian talk and pointed far off to the east and south and back again to me and reached inside the old blanket he had fastened around him with a belt and took out a dirty cloth-wrapped package and laid it at my feet and went away and faded out of sight around the shack. When I unrolled that package there were these moccasins.

Funny thing. I never wanted to go around telling my story to the other boys again. Didn't need to. Whether they believed or not wasn't important anymore. I had those moccasins. In a way they made me one of Jacob's children. Remembering that has helped me sometimes in tough spots.

SALT OF

THE EARTH

ld Clyde Foskins finished milking the one old cow and turned her out into the poled pasture behind the barn where a few clumps of winter-cured grass remained. He tilted the milk from the pail through a strainer into another pail. He carried this out and to the well and pulled on a cord hanging down into the shadowy depth until a large glass mason jar rose dripping from the water. Carefully he unscrewed the top and filled the jar from the pail. Carefully he screwed the top tight again and lowered the jar into the water. He stared down after it, sniffling some through his limp mustache. "Beats any icebox," he said. "Keeps it cold in summer. Keeps it from freezing in winter."

He picked up the pail and went to the pigpen beside the barn and poured the rest of the milk into the tin-lined trough there. He watched the old boar and two unwieldy sows jostle each other for position. "Funny way of doing," he said. "Take it out of one critter and put it right back into some others." He carried the empty pail into the barn and hung it with the other on their regular nails in an overhead beam. He stood peering about the dim interior wrinkling his nose. "Kind of sour. Needs an airing." He pushed and heaved at the wide old main doors and the hangers squealed on the track above and the doors moved and the morning sunlight streamed through the opening.

Old Clyde Foskins stood in the wide doorway and looked across the rutted barnyard at the brown field beyond long since stripped of the last grass tufts and at the horse close behind the rails, still, motionless, a part of the brown country stretching on to the broken gullies that led to the far hills. Gaunt with age, big bones pushing against shrunken hide, the horse stood as if propped on four stiff legs and the big head hung low with its weight, almost touching the ground. Old Clyde whistled through his mustache, sharp and shrill. The big ears of the horse twitched and the head rose a few inches and stopped and sank slowly again. He turned back into the barn and reached with a fork to pull hay from the low loft. He gathered an armful and went out and across the barnyard and dropped it over the rails close by the big head. "Cri-ma-nently!" he said. "Get some interest in life. At least you can still eat." The head moved and the neck stretched and the horse took a mouthful of hay, not in hunger but in old instinctive obedience to do what was wanted. The big jaws ground in slow rhythm working the hay back over worn gums and the nubs of the few remaining teeth.

Old Clyde slapped his hands on the top rail and surveyed the horse from scraggly burr-locked tail to graying bearded muzzle. "You certainly ain't very pretty," he said. "Crow-bait, that's about all. Maybe even they'd pass you by." The horse rolled its eyes towards him till the white of the near one showed plain and he slapped his hands on the top rail again. "Don't go getting worried. It's near to plowing time, certain enough, but I'll not be making you do that. I'll be getting me another one. Maybe two. It'll take two to match what you were." He rubbed his hands along the rail and stared at them and for a moment had trouble seeing them through the mistiness clouding his eyes. "You've done enough for a dozen," he said. He pushed against the rail and straightened his old shoulders. "Company. That'll perk you some." He snorted at himself and at the horse in exasperation. "No. You don't need company. Not at your age." He turned and started across the barnyard ruts towards the small back porch of the silent three-room house. "Like me," he said.

* * *

Sunlight through the kitchen window had reached the crack in the floorboards that meant the general neighborhood of two o'clock. Old Clyde sat at the kitchen table turning and returning the pages of last week's newspaper and worked with slow sips at the last cup of coffee, reheated, half milk the way he liked it, from the pot made for lunch. Old dishes on the shelf above the corner cupboard rattled gently and he looked up and out the window and heard the hoofs first then saw the team of small quick-stepping trotters and then the buggy sagging with the weight of his two stout sons as it slid to a stop in the lane beside the house. He started up in sudden eagerness and put his face close to the glass and dropped back into the chair. "Cri-ma-nently," he said. "Both at once. That means something." He pushed up again, slowly, and went to the door and opened it for them. "Afternoon, Ed. Same, Mert. Find yourselves chairs. Won't take a moment for a fresh pot of coffee."

"Not now, Father." Ed Foskins, owner of the trotters, owner of a smooth fresh face, ruddy with good living, watched his younger brother hurry to the nearest chair and sink his wide shape on it with a sigh. "What's the matter, Mert? That road get you? You're softer than me already." He closed the door and stood with his back against it facing old Clyde. "No time for coffee, Father. I have to be back at the bank by closing. Mert here oughtn't be away from the store. But Lord knows when we'd have another chance to get out here. We want to talk to you."

Old Clyde backed across the room until he felt the sustaining solidity of the table behind him. He was painfully aware of his unshaven face, of his crusted heavy work shoes and stained dungarees and patched flannel shirt. He looked from one to the other of his sons, neat and respectable in their town clothes, and as always pride and regret matched themselves in him. "Go ahead, talk," he said.

Mert shifted for more comfort on his chair. "Ed'll do it. But I agree with him. Absolutely. It's logical. It's right."

"Well, now." Ed Foskins, the glib one, the good talker, swung into stride. "We didn't want to rush you right after the funeral and all. But it's been six months now since Mother was buried—"

"Six months," old Clyde said. "And four days."

"Right. And four days. But you can't go on living way

out here alone. It isn't natural. It doesn't make sense. On an old rundown farm that—"

"It ain't rundown!" Old Clyde's voice shook with indignation. "I had a good corn crop last year, didn't I? Wheat did good too. Paid off my seed loan and some over. You ought to know, you being in the bank."

"Well, yes, sure you did. But you don't need to. That's it. That's the point. No sense a man working when he doesn't need to. You've done your share. All Mert and me can remember when we were boys is you working. All the time. Never any end to it. And you don't need to any more. I checked your account again this morning. You've got better than two thousand. With what you can get for this place, which won't be too much but I can help you get what it's worth, you'd have enough to take it easy in town for—well, for—for as long as—"

"Go ahead, say it!" Old Clyde's voice shook again. "For the little time I've got left you mean. I know that ain't much. I'm your father but I'm old enough to be your grandfather, I got married so damn late." The words were coming and he could not stop them. "Maybe that's why we didn't get along so good, you had to hurry out of here into town soon as you could. Both of you. Maybe I was too old already to be the kind of father you wanted. Well, you wasn't exactly the kind of sons I wanted either. Had to keep after you getting things done around here. Had to do most of it myself. Well, I did it, didn't I? And, well, I'm older now. But I ain't afraid of it." He shifted along the table and around the corner and sank into the chair there and pushed with a shaking finger at his half-empty coffee cup. "Cri-ma-nently! I ain't meaning to get mad. What d'you have to keep worrying about me now for? Whyn't you just let me worry about myself?"

Mert Foskins teetered his bulk forward on his chair. "See, Ed? Still the old rooster. That's what I keep telling Flossie. I want him to move in with us. Pay a little board to help out but that's all. Be good for the kids, the way she keeps spoiling—"

"Shut up, Mert." Ed Foskins, the elder, the leader from boyhood, was in command. He took a deep breath. "Father, you don't understand. We aren't trying to push you into anything. We're just thinking what's good for you. These days people take things easier. There's no sense doing the way you do, rest some in winter and then be at it every daylight hour soon as the ground is soft enough for plowing. Maybe that made sense when it was the only way to get along. These days things are different. How do you think you make Mert and me feel, us doing well in town and you living out here like you didn't have a nickel?" Ed Foskins saw the muscles of old Clyde's face tightening. "Now wait a minute, Father. This is hard to say, to you anyway, but I'm saying it. Maybe now Mert and me are older too and we're realizing a few things we didn't before. We wouldn't be where we are now if you hadn't worked like that. Not many men could do what you did, past fifty already and with a wife and two little kids and having to start all over again with nothing on a piece of poor government land. You raised us and you squawked when we pulled out but all the same you helped us get started in town with what you could and, well, your job's done and it's about time you quit working and took life easy. Mert and me, we—"

Old Clyde was no longer listening. His head was high. He was thinking back twenty-some years. "I had a horse," he said.

He looked out the window past the buggy and the shining young trotters, beyond the fence, at the big gaunt figure propped on four stiff legs, head low, motionless. "I've still got him."

Mert's chair squealed as he straightened on it. "You mean that rack of bones out there is old Mark? I thought he was gone years ago. Must be more'n thirty."

"Twenty-eight," old Clyde said. "Twenty-five years I've had him and twenty-five years he's been doing anything I ever asked of him." Old Clyde's head dropped and he stared down at his coffee cup. "Nearly twenty-five anyway."

"You mean," Ed Foskins was surprised, "you mean you've been thinking of going right on farming and with that old horse?"

"No!" Old Clyde pushed his coffee cup clattering on its saucer. He looked up at Ed half apologetic, half defiant. "Not that horse. He's done his share. Gave out on me one day last fall and more'n about time the way I see it. I been figuring to get another one. Maybe a team. Herb Calloway towards town has a few for sale." He grabbed the cup and gulped the cold remainder of his coffee and wiped his mustache. "No siree bob, that horse ain't going to do another

day's work. He's earned his rest. He's going to get plenty
to eat and loaf around and take it easy and—" Old Clyde
stopped, startled at his own words.

"That's right!" Ed Foskins jumped at the chance. "That's
exactly what we mean. You've earned your rest too. You're
going to loaf around and take it easy and let somebody else,
me and Marilyn or Mert and Flossie or likely both of us in
turn, take care of you and see you get decent meals. You're
going to quit working and do just what you feel like doing
and not a damn thing else. You said it yourself. You've
earned it."

Old Clyde felt trapped and by his own reasoning and this
time he felt no answering urge to pull free. He was suddenly
aware of what he had kept hidden, even from himself, the
tiredness deep in him, the desire to be still, like the big
gaunt figure out by the fence, head low, doing nothing. "I
don't know," he said. "I been getting muddled, off and on,
lately. Never could figure things quick like you, Ed." He
slumped lower on the chair and felt the tiredness taking
him. "But I'd just be a nuisance around."

"Sure you would. But so what?" Ed Foskins, the first
rebel, the sound at heart, grinned in remembrance. "Me and
Mert were nuisances to you. Turn-about's fair enough."

"No," old Clyde said. "I can't do it. There's that horse—"

Mert's chair squealed again. "Old Mark? Him too. There's
a field back of my place. Won't cost much to rent it."

"Well, then," Ed said, quickly. "That's settled. That's
the way to do things, make up your mind and do them.
Suppose you move in with Mert first. My new place isn't
finished yet and he has more room right now. You'll be
wanting a little time to get used to the idea. Suppose we
make it week after next. Monday. I'll send a wagon . . ."

Old Clyde Foskins stood on his little back porch and
watched the buggy back and swing and move out of the lane
into the road. There was an ache in his throat, a tightness
no gulping could ease. "I didn't know they felt that way,"
he said. He watched the buggy dwindle into the distance
and drop out of sight beyond the first rolling ridge. "Maybe
Ed's right. Maybe Ed's been right all along. Certainly doing
well." He saw the buggy, small, a moving dot in the distance,
top the second and higher rolling ridge and disappear beyond
towards town. He turned slowly and looked at his old out-

buildings and the leaning fences in ragged lines between his
fields. "It is kind of rundown. Needs a lot of fixing. No sense
doing that now."

The water was hot on the stove, steaming in the bucket
and making it wobble on the rusty burner. Old Clyde sloshed
some into the dishpan and did up his breakfast dishes with
a minimum of soap and effort. He rubbed one hand around
his chin and felt the stubble there. "Cri-ma-nently," he said.
"Must be a week, ten days, since I shaved last. Time's coming and they'll be wanting to slick me some. Might as well
get in practice." He sloshed more water into a basin and set
this on the chest-high shelf by the window. He rooted around
in the corner cupboard until he found his nubbin of a brush
and his old straight-edge. He put these with a small square
mirror on the shelf beside the basin and went to work on
his whiskers. He pulled at the loose skin under his chin to
stretch out the wrinkles and let the blade catch the bristles.
"Kind of a silly business," he said. "Most natural thing in
the world for a man to have hair on his face. Wouldn't feel
a man without it. Yet right away they have to come off."
He rooted in the cupboard again and found a pair of old
scissors and went back by the shelf and started trimming
his mustache. "Got to be more particular. Bird could build
a nest in this thing." Suddenly he pulled back and stared at
himself hard in the mirror. "Talking to myself. How long've
I been doing that?" He shrugged his old shoulders and grabbed
the flour sacking that served for a towel and rubbed his face
vigorously. "Ain't nobody's business but my own anyway."
He tossed the flour sacking on the table. "But it will be.
Have to quit it come next Monday."

He was reaching to gather the things on the shelf when
he caught a glimpse of movement through the window. He
shifted to see more clearly. Out in the field, just beyond the
fence, the big gaunt figure was moving. Head up, sniffing
the air, stiff and awkward with age, the old horse was walking along the fence line. It reached the gate opposite the
barn and stopped and looked over. It turned and came back
to the familiar resting spot opposite the house and turned
and started up along the fence line again.

Old Clyde watched, his eyebrows twitching upward. "Well,
now," he said, "look at him perking some. Must be a touch
of spring." He went out on his little back porch and sniffed

the air himself. The unending wind was strong and chill but faint along its edges was the old eternal promise. He drew in a deep breath. "It's there. Snow's been gone about three weeks. Dampness going. A man figuring on some planting would be getting the ground ready." He sighed softly. "Not me. Mighty nice not to have that hanging over me any more. Sit all day if I feel like it."

Inside, by the stove, old Clyde soaked up warmth and began to leaf through his pile of farm journals for the articles he had always intended to read but never got around to. He read slowly, sometimes following the lines with a blunt forefinger, mumbling the words to himself, agreeing and disagreeing with what he read. The sun inched across the kitchen floor and he hitched his chair along to follow it. And outside the wind blew and carried its ancient message and the sun shone and the old horse stood in its resting place opposite the house, head low, motionless, and now and again raised its head and sniffed and walked, slow and ungainly with the wind ruffling its long winter hair, up along the fence line to look over the gate opposite the barn and swing around and return.

Old Clyde fidgeted on his chair. Suddenly he dropped the journal he was holding. "Got things to do. Might as well get at them." He went to the dusty telephone on the front room wall and took down the earpiece and cranked the handle on the side. He gave his number and waited a moment and then, as always, put his mouth close and shouted. "Mrs. Calloway? Clyde Foskins down the road. You tell Herb I've got a cow and some pigs to sell him. You tell him to be here right after lunch or I'll sell 'em to somebody else."

Herb Calloway finished fastening the tail gate of his big stock wagon. He climbed to the driving seat and waved a cheery farewell. He clucked to his team of plump young workhorses and they surged willingly into the traces. Old Clyde watched the wagon turn into the road and start its steady rolling into the distance. The sun was so warm on his bare head and old jacket that he settled himself on the edge of the back porch to enjoy it. He chuckled softly to himself. "These younger ones don't know how to bargain any more. Got eleven dollars more'n the top I figured on getting."

Out in the field, just beyond the fence, the old horse had

turned, head up, to watch the young team go past. It swung around and started up along the fence line and broke into a lumbering trot. It stopped by the gate opposite the barn and looked over. Old Clyde studied it, eyebrows twitching. "What you so all-fired interested in that barn for? There's hay out there if you want it." He moved a bit to look at the old barn straight on and saw that the wind was swaying one of the big main doors and that the wood at the top was rotten and the hangers were tearing loose. "Well, now, ain't that too bad," he said. "Can't argue I'll be sorry to leave this rundown old place, everything falling apart." He let his breath out in a long sigh. "Mighty nice not to have to be doing things all the time. Just what I feel like doing. Right now I feel like sitting."

He sat in the sun and watched the old horse go back down the fence line, wait a moment, turn and go up again and stop by the gate, and swing yet again and repeat the maneuver, over and over. "Cri-ma-nently!" He stood up. "If you want some exercise, why keep following that fence? You've got a whole damn field to move around in." He walked towards the barn and stood staring up at the creaking door. "Shucks. Might as well fix that anyway. Can't get a good price, things falling apart."

The wind blew, steady and chill but with a softness blunting its bite, and fiddled with the edges of the loosened worn shingles old Clyde was renailing on the barn roof. The morning sun was warm on his back. He fastened the last shingle and inched, crablike, down the slope to the ladder. Rung by rung he descended, moving slowly, calculating each step like a man who knows his muscles have lost their snap and he must use what strength he has carefully, spread out over a job. On the ground, he straightened himself, wincing a little at the twinges in his back. He looked up the ladder. "Well, now," he said, "that ought to be worth fifty dollars more on the price."

He went around and through the wide open doorway and hung his old hammer on the wall between its two nails. He stood in the doorway and saw the big gaunt figure in the field moving, moving, slowly, steadily, up the fence line and stop and down and return, wearing ever deeper into the pathway already worn. Suddenly an anger, out of nowhere, forced his voice into a shout. "Stop it! What's got into you?"

The old horse had reached the gate opposite the barn again. It looked over and across the barnyard at him. One big forefoot rose and pawed at the lowest rail. There was a small crackling sound and little splinters broke from the wood. Old Clyde stared and as he stared the anger dwindled in him.

He went towards the gate and the old horse raised its head higher and whiffled softly at him and pressed its chest forward against the top rail. "Mark," he said. "Mark boy. You want out? What in hell for?" He felt a strange light-headedness, a deliberate emptiness of thought. He stepped forward, hardly aware what he was doing, and the horse stepped back and he tugged at the rails till they fell at his feet. Head high, breathing deeply, the old horse stepped over them and past him. Straight to the barn it went and in through the wide doorway. He followed. He stood in the doorway and saw it standing, waiting, motionless, patient, by the harness rack, and seeing he felt the anger flare and fill him, strong and bitter. "So you think you've still got it in you! I'll show you! You couldn't drag it ten feet!" With trembling, hurrying fingers he snatched the old bridle with its long driving reins from its peg and jammed the rusty bit between the big old waiting jaws. He grabbed the harness and threw it over the big bony frame. He fought with the buckles to fasten them and cursed at the clumsiness of haste. He took the reins and slapped with the loose ends hard at the horse's rump and swung it around and backed it to where the old plow lay on the barn floor. He fastened the tugs with sharp jerks, muttering steadily under his breath. He took the reins again and slapped again with the loose ends. "All right, get moving! I'll show you! I'll show you good!"

Head high, ears forward, the old horse moved and the old plow clattered on its side along the rough floor planks and old Clyde walked beside it. Out of the barn, around the pigpen, past the empty back pasture, to the wide spreading rear field where the corn stubble marked its old rows with withered tufted weeds and grass between. Old Clyde's voice rose, still in anger but with a note of frantic appeal. "Cri-ma-nently! Ain't I been telling you? You're too old! There ain't any sense to it! Wait'll you hit the dirt! Wait'll the 'share digs in! That'll show you!"

He yanked on the reins and the old horse stopped, leaning its weight slightly forward into the harness to hold the tugs tight. Quickly, with the sureness of old habit, he knotted the rein ends together and flipped the loop over his head and around his shoulders. He leaned and took hold of the plow handles and struggled with them until the plow was upright, ready. "Giddap!" he yelled. "Yank your goddamn heart out! That'll learn you!" The old horse surged forward and as it moved old Clyde heaved up on the handles so that the blade pointed into the ground. Smoothly, surely, the blade sank in and leveled for the straight pull and stopped against the hard mass of the subsoil. He heard the breath of the old horse wheeze in its throat and saw the ribs straining through the shaggy hide and the old cracked hoofs digging into the dirt—and the plow moved, slow, hesitating, forward and stop and forward again and not stopping and the clean earth rolled from the moldboard and lay in a darkened ribbon by the fresh furrow beside his plodding feet.

Slowly, unsteadily, but always forward, concentrating with an intense earnestness, the horse and the man with the plow biting into the earth between them crawled along the length of the wide spreading field.

They stopped at the far end and old Clyde turned his head to look back along the furrow. "Cri-ma-nently," he said softly. "Straight as a string." He jerked his head around and pulled quickly on the plow to free the blade from the ground, for the old horse, breathing heavily, was moving again, was starting to swing in the arc that would bring them around for the return trip back along the field. He fought with the plow to get it turned in time and pulled it upright and heaved quickly on the handles so they would not lose the forward momentum and the blade sank into the ground and leveled and the new furrow began to unroll. And suddenly he was no longer an old man plodding along, plowing often-plowed ground behind an old gaunt horse that struggled with each forward step, whose big old bones thrust out against shrunken hide. He was a man with a snap still in his knees, striding along, striding behind a huge young horse, filled out, great-muscled, sleek with sweat, big head slogging forward into the terrific strain as the plow sliced deep through the tangled matted roots of virgin prairie sod. "Yippee!" he yelled. "Smash into it, Mark boy! I know what people are saying. That Foskins is a damn fool. He'll never make it. Have to have oxen or a four-horse span to break that ground. I ain't got those. But I've got you, boy! We'll show 'em!" He was striding along, feet striking firm beside the furrow, striding along behind huge young Mark, the tireless, the indomitable, great heart driving great muscles, plowing forward through unending resistant sod, through the days and the weeks and the months, and the sweat of their work salted the earth of the years.

Old Clyde Foskins realized he was standing still, gripping the plow handles so hard that his fingers hurt. The plow had stopped. Ahead of him the old horse wavered on four stiff legs and shudders ran through its body and its breath whistled shrill in its throat. The big head sank lower and lower and the big gaunt frame crumpled and toppled forward and sideways and to the ground and the weight dragging on the harness pulled the plow over on its side.

Carefully old Clyde lifted the knotted reins over his head and dropped them. He went around by the still figure and looked down. The eyes were open, staring, and there was no life in them. He stood quietly, looking down, for a long time. "It'll take a mighty big hole," he said. He raised his head and looked out along the fresh furrows. "I expect a corner of this field'll be about right. It's as much his as mine." He stood quietly, staring into the distance. He raised one calloused old hand and brushed it across his eyes to clear the mistiness from them. "Yes," he said. "Yes. He was right. That's the way to do it."

He walked, slowly and steadily, out of the field, past the empty back pasture, around the empty pigpen, across the barnyard, up on his little back porch and into the house. He went straight to the dusty telephone on the front room wall and took down the earpiece and cranked the handle. He gave his number and waited. He put his mouth close and shouted. "Marilyn? You tell Ed when he gets home I don't want any wagon on Monday. Or any time." Quickly he pushed down the receiver hook with a finger and waited again. After a moment he released the hook and cranked the handle once more and gave his number. He put his mouth close and shouted. "Mrs. Calloway? You tell Herb I'll be there to see him shortly. Want to dicker for a couple of horses."

He pulled his old jacket closer about him and went out on his little back porch. He heard the telephone ringing behind him, three rings, his call. "Let 'em keep that thing buzzing all day," he said. "I ain't got time to argue. Got my spring plowing to do." He went around the house and along the lane. "That team Herb had here yesterday. The two of them together might do. Maybe buy back that cow too. She always gave down good for me." Walking slowly and steadily, he headed up the road.

ONE MAN'S

HONOR

This happened out where distance ran past vision and only clumped silver-green of sagebrush and blunt bare rising ridges of rock broke the red-brown reaches of sand and sun-baked silt. No highways or railroads sliced it into measurable stretches. Only a lone rutted trace snaked through, following the lower levels, worn by freighters who crawled at long intervals with their clumsy wagons from the last meager town far southward on the river to the rolling cattle ranges far northward on the more fertile uplands. Yet here and there, off the trace, widely separated and hidden between the ridges where slow short-season streams made narrow areas of green before dying in the sand, the first settlers had come. They would increase and windmills would rise to draw upon the subsurface water and in time a network of roads would fan out and wheels would grind dust for hot winds to whirl. Now they were few and far, lost in the immensity of distance and red-brown desolation under the limitless depth of sky.

Late afternoon sun slanted over one of the higher ridges and shone on the sparse beginnings of a homestead claim.

Clear and hot in the clean air, it shone on a long strip of shallow-plowed ground that followed the gradual curve of an almost-dry stream bed where a few brackish pools lingered and on a sagging pole corral where an old milk cow and two stocky ungainly draft horses drooped in motionless rest and beside this on the shelter, half dugout cut into the rise of a small ground swell, half timbered with scrub logs from the stunted cottonwoods that straggled along the other side of the stream bed. Trimmed branches corded together and plastered over with clay formed the roof and a rusting stovepipe rose from it. On the split-log doorstep sat a little girl. Her short scratched sunburned legs barely reached the ground. Her light brown hair, sun-bleached in lighter streaks, curled softly down to frame a round snub-nosed face whose dark eyes, unmasked by the light lashes, were wide and bright. A twenty-foot length of rope was tied around her waist and fastened to a staple driven into the doorjamb. She was small and serious and very quiet and she smoothed the skirt of her small flour-sacking dress down over her bare knees and poked, earnest and intent, one small moccasined foot at an ant scurrying in the dooryard dust.

Behind her, in the dim recess of the one-windowed shelter, a tall flat-bodied man stooped over a rumpled bed against the rear wall and laid a moistened cloth across the forehead of a woman lying there. His voice was low and harsh with irritation but the touch of his hand was gentle. "What's got into ye?" he said.

The woman stared up at him, apology plain on her thin flushed face. "I don't know," she whispered. "It just came on me sudden-like." Her thin body under the patched gingham of her dress shook with slight tremors as with a chill yet drops of sweat streaked her cheeks. Her voice came faint and wavering. "You'll have to do the food. There's soup in the kettle."

The man brushed one hand impatiently at the flies hovering over the bed. "Ye'll be better in the morning," he said. Abruptly he turned and went to the stove set against the right wall. The woman watched him. She tried to speak and could not. She lay still a moment and summoned strength to rise on her elbows and send her voice across the room to him. "Wait," she said. "Wait. You'll have to do the game with her. It's her fun. It helps her learn."

The man swung his head to look at the doorway. The

little girl sat still, her back to him, her head bent forward as she peered at something by her feet. The last sun slanting over the ridge filtered through the tangled curls along her neck. Slowly the lines of worry and irritation faded from the man's face and the tightness around his mouth eased. He went to the doorway and leaned low to untie the rope around her waist. She stood up, small and soft beside his hard height, and stretched back her head to look up at him. She raised one small hand and reached to put it in one of his big calloused hands. Together they went along the front of the shelter towards the corral.

Near the corner the man stopped. He slapped his free hand on the side of the shelter. "This," he said.

Gravely the little girl regarded the shelter. A triumphant smile crinkled her small face. "Hello, house," she said.

"Right," the man said. They moved on and stopped by an old wagon pulled in close alongside the shelter. The man reached under and pulled out an empty milk pail and held it up. Gravely the little girl regarded it. Her small eyebrows drew down in a frown. She looked up at the man in doubt and back at the object in his hand. "Hello," she said slowly, "hello, buck-et."

"That's it!" The man grinned down at her and reached to put the pail back under the wagon. They moved on to the sagging poles of the corral. The man pointed over the poles at the cow and the little girl peered through them beside him. She spoke at once, quick and proud. "Hello, cow."

"What's the cow's name?"

"Bess-ie."

"Mighty smart ye're getting to be," the man said. He pointed over the poles at the draft horses standing together in a corner.

The little girl tossed her head. "Hello, horse."

"No," the man said. "There's two of them. More than one. Horses."

The little girl looked up at him, small and earnest and intent. She looked back through the poles across the corral. "Hello, horses."

Forty-three miles to the south and five miles west of the meager town on the river, where the ground dipped in a hollow some ten feet below the level expanse around, a saddled horse stood alone, ground-reined, patiently waiting. A

wide-brimmed weather-worn hat hung on the saddle horn.
Several hundred yards away the river road followed the
bank, a dust track running west into fading distance and
east towards the low hills hiding the town. Close by the
roadside two small rocks jutted out of the ground, butted
against each other. Together they were little more than
three feet wide, irregular in shape, no more than eighteen
inches high at the highest point. The late afternoon sun
slanted down on them and they made a small lengthening
patch of shade. Beside them, stretched out, head and shoulders into the shade, a man lay flat, belly down, pressed
against the ground. Beside him lay a rifle. Its barrel had
been rubbed with dirt to remove all shine. He was a short
man, short and thick, with a head that seemed small, out of
proportion to the thick body, set too close into the hunched
shoulders. His hair was a dirty black, close-cropped with
the rough scissor slashes of his own cutting plainly marked,
and it merged with no visible break into the dark unshaven
stubble down his cheeks and around his narrow tight-lipped
mouth.

He raised his head higher to sight along the road to the
west through the cleft where the tops of the two rocks joined.
Pushing with his toes in beaten scarred old knee-length boots,
he hitched his body a few inches to the left so that it lay
almost exactly parallel to the road, invisible to anyone approaching in the distance from the west. As he moved, the
hammer of the revolver in a holster at his side made a tiny
groove in the ground and he reached to test the firmness of
its seat in the holster and free it of any clinging dirt. His
voice was a low murmur lost in the vast empty reaches of
space, the flat inflectionless voice of a man accustomed to
being alone and to talking to himself. "Last place they'd be
expecting trouble," he said.

He lay flat, his head relaxed on its side with one ear
against the ground, and the sun dropped slowly down the
sky and the patch of shade of the rocks spread down his
back and reached the brass-studded cartridge belt around
his waist and far out along the road to the west a tiny puff
of dust appeared and crept closer, barely seeming to move
only to grow imperceptibly larger in the angled foreshorten-
ing of distance. Faint tremors in the ground came to the
man's ear. He raised his head and sighted through the rock
cleft. He rolled on his side and pulled the tattered old ban-

danna tied loosely around his neck up over his face, up to
the bridge of his nose so that only his eyes and forehead
showed over it. He rolled back into position and took the
rifle and eased the barrel forward through the cleft. Propped
on his elbows with the curved butt of the rifle against his
right shoulder and his right cheek under the bandanna against
the stock, he watched the puff of dust far out along the road.

It was no longer just a puff of dust. Emerging from it
yet never escaping and always emerging as the dust rose
under the hoofs was a light fast freight wagon drawn by two
stout horses at a steady trot. Two men sat on the board-
backed seat, the driver and another man with a shotgun
between his knees, the butt on the floorboard, the barrel
pointing at the sky.

The man behind the rocks waited. He waited until the
wagon was little more than one hundred feet away and in a
few seconds he would begin to be visible over the top of the
rocks and his finger tightened on the trigger of the rifle and
with the crash of the shot the man with the shotgun jolted
hard against the back of the wagon seat and the horses
reared, beating upward with their front hoofs and trying to
swing away, and the man with the shotgun dropped it clattering on the floorboard and struggled to stand on the swaying platform and toppled sideways into the road dust and
lay still.

The man behind the rocks let the rifle stock fall to the
ground and leaped up and in the leaping took the revolver
from the holster at his side. He moved out and around the
rocks and closer to the wagon and watched the driver fighting with the horses to quiet them. He watched the driver
pull them to quivering stillness and become aware of him
and the gun in his hand and stiffen in a tight silence. "That's
right," he said. "Keep your hands on those reins where I
can see them." He moved closer and to the right side of the
wagon and with his left hand took the shotgun from the
floorboard and tossed it back from the road. He moved out
and around the horses to the left side of the wagon and took
the driver's revolver from its holster and threw it towards
the river. He stepped back, away from the wagon. "Now,"
he said. "Take it slow. Wrap the reins around that brake.
Put your hands up behind your head." The driver hesitated.
His lips were pale, pressed tight together, and a slow flush
crept up his cheeks. He reached slowly and looped the reins

over the brake handle and raised his hands and clasped them together at the back of his head.

The man with the gun stepped up by the body of the wagon. He was careful to stand facing part way forward so that the driver was always within his angle of vision. With his left hand he unfastened the rope lashed over the wagon and pulled away the light canvas dust cover. Four square boxes and several small crates and a half-dozen sacks of potatoes were exposed to view. He chuckled, a strange harsh sound in the wide silence. "Mighty little load to be packing a guard," he said. He swung his head for a quick check of the load and back to look straight at the driver. His voice was suddenly sharp and biting. "Where is it? I know you're carrying it." The driver had pivoted his body at the hips to watch him and stared at him and said nothing.

The man with the gun grunted and reached with his left hand to yank aside one of the sacks of potatoes. He reached again and heaved to move aside the one that had been beneath the first. He plunged the hand into the hole opened to the bed of the wagon and felt around and pulled out a small metal box. He stepped back and again his strange harsh chuckle sounded in the silence.

The voice of the driver broke through the tight line of his lips. "You'll never get away with it, Kemp. I'd know that gunbelt anywhere."

The man with the gun let the metal box fall from his left hand and lifted the hand and pulled the bandanna down from his face. "Too bad," he said. He raised his right hand and the gun in it bucked with the shot and the driver rose upright off the seat arching his back in sudden agony and fell sideways over the footboard to strike on the wagon tongue and bounce to the ground between the harness tugs and with the roar of the shot the horses were rearing and they plunged ahead and the wheels crunched over the driver's body as they rolled forward along the road.

The man with the gun took one leap after the wagon and stopped. He raised the gun again and in almost aimless haste fired the four remaining bullets in it at the plunging horses. The horses drove forward, goaded by several flesh wounds, and the reins ripped off the brake handle and the wagon careened after them and swerved to the left and the left front wheel struck against the rocks behind which the man had been hiding. The wagon bounced upward as the wheel cracked and the harness tugs snapped and the horses, freed of the weight, surged in frantic gallop along the road.

The man threw the empty revolver to the ground. He raced to the wagon and around it to the rocks and leaped over them and grabbed the rifle. He dropped to his right knee and braced his left elbow on his left knee to steady his aim and fired and one of the horses staggered and fell and the other, pulled sideways by the falling weight, lashed frantically with its hoofs and the harness parted and the horse galloped ahead alone along the road. Already it was a far shape, dwindling into distance, and the man fired again and again until the magazine of the rifle was emptied and the bullets kicked small spurts of dust and the horse galloped on unhit into the low hills. The man threw down the rifle and stood erect. He was shaking with a tense fury. He stood still, forcing himself to quiet, driving the shaking out of his body. He drew a long breath. "That'll tell 'em too damn soon," he said. Quickly he took up the rifle and opened the breech and blew through the barrel and loaded the magazine with bullets from the pocket of his faded old shirt. He hurried back where he had dropped the metal box. The two bodies lay near in the road dust and already the flies were gathering and he paid no attention to them. He picked up the revolver and loaded it with bullets from the brass-studded belt around his waist. He reached down and blasted the lock of the metal box with a single shot and ripped the top open and took out two small plump leather bags and a sheaf of bills and jammed these into the pockets of his old patched pants. At a steady run he moved away from the road, across the level expanse, to the hollow several hundred yards away and the waiting horse. With swift sure gestures he slapped the hat on his head and pushed the rifle into its saddle scabbard and transferred the two small bags and the bills to the saddlebag. He swung up and yanked the horse around, lifting it into a fast lope, and headed north through the red-brown reaches of distance.

Early morning sun slanted in from the east on the homestead shelter. It made a narrow triangular patch of brightness on the packed dirt floor through the open doorway and pushed a soft glow further into the room. On the edge of a low short trundle cot against the back wall by the foot of the big bed the little girl sat, her body bent forward, her small face puckered in a frown as she concentrated on the problem of putting the right little moccasin on the right foot. On the bed itself the woman lay thin and motionless. Her eyes were closed. At intervals the eyelids twitched and flickered and were still. Her mouth was partly open and her breath drew through it in long slow straining gasps. On the floor beside the bed, stretched on an old quilt folded over, the man lay asleep, fully dressed except for his short thick boots.

The little girl finished with the moccasins. She slid to the floor and turned and tried to smooth the old blanket on her cot. She took hold of the cot and tugged at it to pull it a few inches out from the wall. She went to the end of it away from the bed and turned her small back to it and against it and pushed with her feet to move it along the floor and slide it under the bed.

The scratching sound of the cot runners scraping on the hard dirt floor roused the man. He bent his body at the waist to sit up and wavered and fell back. He pushed against the floor with both hands and was up to sitting position. He looked around, his eyes glassy and staring, and saw the boots and his attention focused on them and he reached for them and struggled to get them on. He heaved himself over on one hip and pushed against the floor and stood swaying on his feet. Sweat streamed down his face and his body shook as with a chill. He took a step and staggered and fell towards the wall and clutched at it for support. He moved along it to the head of the bed. Leaning his weight on one hand on the bed, he reached with the other to the woman's shoulder and gently shook her. Her head wobbled limply at the pressure and her eyes remained closed. He straightened against the wall. Slowly he wiped one hand down over his damp face and let it fall to his side.

The little girl stood by the foot of the bed and looked up at him. Slowly his attention focused on her. He stared at her for a long moment and she looked up at him and a small smile of greeting touched her face and was gone. He drew a long slow sobbing breath and by sheer effort of will pushed out from the wall. His feet dragged and he moved in a strange lurching walk. He took the old quilt from the floor and reached under the bed to take the old blanket from the cot and pulled a pile of empty flour sacks down from a shelf. With these in his arms he staggered to the doorway and out and along the

front of the shelter to the old wagon beside it. He heaved
his load into the body of the wagon and leaned panting on
the side to reach in and spread out the sacks and put the
blanket and quilt over them. Weakness took him and he
swayed against one of the wagon wheels and hung over it
while sweat dripped in tiny glistening beads from his chin
to the ground below. He pushed out from the wheel and
veered to the shelter wall and hitched his way along towards
the door. The little girl was in the doorway and she backed
away inside and he held to the doorjamb and pulled himself
around and in and a short way along the inside wall and
reached for the team harness hanging on two wooden pegs
and in the reaching suddenly sagged in a limp helplessness
and collapsed doubling forward to bump against the wall and
slide to the floor. His body stretched out and rolled over
and his unseeing eyes stared upward a few seconds and the
lids dropped and no motion stirred in him except the long
slow heaving of his chest.

The little girl stared at the man lying still and silent and
her eyebrows drew together in a frown. She looked at the
woman on the bed and back at the man on the floor. She
turned away and went to the table under the one window
in the right wall and climbed on the chair beside it and then
onto the table. Standing on tiptoe and leaning out she reached
one hand into an earthenware jar on the shelf by the window
and took it out with a cracker clutched in her fingers. She
climbed down to the chair and sat on it with her short sunburned legs swinging over the edge. Gravely she regarded
the object in her hand. "Hello, crack-er," she said in a soft
hushed voice. Gravely she bit off a corner and began to chew
it.

A mile and a half to the southeast the early morning sun
sent long shadows streaming out from a man and a horse
climbing the rough slope of a twisting boulder-strewn ridge.
The man rode with his short thick body hunched forward
and the sun glinted on the brass studdings of the cartridge
belt around his waist. The horse was sweat-streaked, tired,
taking the slope in short spurts as the man kicked it forward.

They topped the ridge and dropped a short way down
the near side and stopped. The man swung to the ground.
He took off his weather-worn hat and slapped at himself
with it to knock some of the dust off his clothes and hung

it on the saddle horn. He turned back to the top of the ridge and lay flat on the blunt bare rock to peer over. No motion anywhere disturbed the empty distance. He turned his head to look at the horse standing with braced legs apart, head hanging, grateful for the rest. He settled himself more comfortably on the rock and watched over the ridge top. The shadows of the boulders down the slope shrank slightly as the sun crept upward and far out along his back trail around a swelling shoulder of wind-piled sand a straggling line of seven tiny figures crawled into view. "Damn funny," he said in a flat inflectionless voice. "Can't shake 'em."

The seven tiny figures crawled closer, increasing in size, seeming to increase in pace as the distance dwindled, and they were seven men on horseback, six in a ragged relatively compact group and one alone in the lead.

The man on the ridge top shaded his eyes against the slant sun and studied the figure in the lead, distinguishable now across the dwindling distance, a lean long-armed figure wearing a buckskin shirt, slim and straight in the saddle on a tall gray horse. He wore no hat and his hair, iron-gray and long, caught the sun clearly in the bobbing rhythm of riding. He rode at a fast trot and at intervals pulled his horse to a brief walk and leaned in the saddle to check the ground beside and ahead.

The man on the ridge top smacked a clenched fist on the rock. "That's it," he said. "Thought he'd left for the mines." He licked his dry lips and spat out the dust-dirty saliva. "Can't just keep running," he said. "Not with him after." He crawled down from the ridge top a few feet and turned squatting on his heels to look down the near slope. Down where it slipped into level expanse of red-brown ground and sparse silver-green of sagebrush, a few-score feet out from the base, a stony dry stream bed followed the twisting formation of the ridge. To the right, swinging in along the level from around a curving twist of the ridge and cutting across the dry stream bed to push in a long arc towards a far break in the next ridge, ran the wagon trace. Plain in the sand dust of the trace, visible from the height, were the day-old unending ribbon ruts of wheel tracks and the hoofprints of many horses heading north.

The man's eyes brightened. He leaped down the slope to his horse and took the rifle from the saddle scabbard and was back on his belly at the ridge top. The seven figures,

suddenly larger, made grotesque in the clear clean brightness of sun by the long shadows streaming sideways from
them, were little more than half a mile away. Deliberately,
in slow succession, careless of exact aim at the range, he
fired once at the figure in the lead and twice at the group
behind and a strange harsh chuckle came from him as he
saw them scatter and swing their horses and gallop back
and cluster again in a jumble around the lean man on the
gray horse. "That'll do it," he said. "They'll take time working up this hill." He pulled back from the ridge top and ran
to the horse and jammed the rifle into the scabbard and
slammed the hat on his head and swung into the saddle. At
a hard run he drove the horse angling down the slope, across
the first few-score feet of level stretch, across the dry stream
bed and angling on across the level to the wagon trace.

He rode along the trace thirty feet, forty, and eased the
horse to a slow stop. Holding it steady, headed north, he
backed it along the trace, back to where he had angled in
and past, back to the crossing of the dry stream bed. Gripping the reins short and pulling up hard on the horse's head
so that it rose on its hind legs, front hoofs pawing the air,
he yanked its head savagely to the left and slammed the
heels of his heavy old boots into its flanks and it leaped,
twisting sideways, and was off the trace on the dry stones
of the stream bed and he clamped down hard on the reins
to hold it from breaking into a surging gallop. Head bent to
one side, peering down in steady concentration, he walked
the horse along the stream bed, picking his way, holding to
the side where the rolled loose stone lay thickest.

He turned his head to look back and up at the ridge top
where he had been. Faintly, over the high rock, came the
sound of a shot and then another. He looked ahead where
the stream bed, following the ridge, curved left with it and
disappeared from sight. He urged the horse into a trot and
he was around the bend, out of sight of the wagon trace
behind. He pulled the horse to the right and out of the stream
bed and on the easier sand-silt ground he pushed it into a
lope, moving west as the ground rose and swinging northwestward as it dropped again.

The morning sun, higher now, shone clear and hot on
the homestead shelter and beat slanting against the high
ridge behind and beyond. A quarter of a mile away, up past

the long shallow-plowed strip by the almost dry stream bed, close in by the base of the ridge, a man sat, short and thick and hunched in the saddle, on a tired sweat-streaked horse. He held the wide brim of his weather-worn hat low over his eyes with one hand as he studied the whole scene before him. Not a sound that he could hear disturbed the empty silence. Not a living thing moved anywhere in sight except the two horses and the old cow in the corral twitching in patient endurance at the flies. He dropped the hand from his hat and reached to take the rifle from its scabbard and hold it ready across the saddle in front of him. He urged the horse into a slow walk, along the base of the ridge and swinging to come to the shelter from the rear.

Fifty feet from the low blank rear wall of the shelter he stopped the horse and dismounted. Quietly he slipped the rifle back into the scabbard and took off his hat and hung it on the saddle horn and in the same gesture flowing onward took the revolver from the holster at his side. Quietly he walked to the rear wall of the shelter. He moved along the rear wall to the right corner and leaned to peer around and then to look across the short space at the corral. He saw that the horses were heavy draft animals and he shook his head in disgust and he saw the swelling udders of the cow, and a puzzled frown showed through the dark stubble on his face and the cow, sighting him, pressed against the poles of the corral and lowed with a soft sighing moan. At the sound he leaped back, close against the rear wall, and the empty silence regained and held and he relaxed and moved again, forward and around the corner.

He was moving past the wagon drawn in by the side of the shelter when he stopped and dropped below the wagon level and listened. Faint, from inside the shelter, he heard a slow creaking sound, then again and yet again and continuing in slow steady rhythm. He waited. The sound stopped and in the silence there was another sound, not heard, below hearing, sensed or felt, and the slow creaking began again and continued, deliberate, unhurried. Cautiously he moved, forward, around the front corner, along the blank wall towards the open doorway. Half crouched, gun raised and ready, he swung swiftly around the doorjamb and into the doorway and there, halfway across the room and confronting him, perched on the seat edge of an old rocking chair and swinging her small body to make the chair roll on its rockers, was a little girl. Caught, rigid in a kind of frantic immobility, he stared at her and her eyes widened at the sight of him and her small body stiffened, swaying gently to the dying motion of the chair. Gravely she regarded him. Her lips lifted slightly in a suggestion of a smile. "Hello, man," she said.

Slowly he straightened. He turned his head and saw the woman motionless on the bed and the man limp on the floor and heard the other sound, audible now inside the room, the long slow unconscious gaspings for breath. He looked back at the little girl and suddenly he was aware of the gun in his hand and he turned his body sidewise to her and as he turned, his head remained towards her swiveling on his short thick neck, and with a quick furtive motion he slid the gun into its holster. He stood still a long moment, his head fixed in its sidelong tipped slant over his shoulder, and looked down at her and gravely she watched him and he seemed unable to look away. Abruptly he jerked his head around straight, swinging his eyes to inspect the room. He went to the shelf by the one window and took a nearly empty flour sack from the floor beneath and laid this on the table. He reached to the shelf and snatched the few cans there and dropped them into the sack.

He stopped, silent and tense, his jaws clenched together, the cords in his neck standing out in strain. He swung around and leaned against the table and jutted his head forward and down at her. His voice struck at her with an angry intensity. "There'll be people coming! They'll untangle my trail! They'll get here sometime!" She stared at him, understanding or not understanding unknown on her face, and he pulled himself around and scooped the bag off the table. He strode to the doorway and out and along the front wall of the shelter and around and back to his horse. He jammed the old hat on his head and fumbled in the saddlebag until he found a short piece of cord and with this tied the flour sack close up to the saddle horn. He mounted and the horse, stronger for the rest, responded as he pulled it around and headed off northwestward, angling towards the high ridge.

He rode slowly, head down, hunched in the saddle, letting the horse find its own pace. There was no urging along the reins, no drumming of heels on its flanks, and the horse stopped. The man sat still in the saddle. He drew a long breath and let it out with a sighing sound. His voice came, flat, inflectionless. "Maybe they won't," he said. Suddenly an explosive fury seemed to burst inside him and strike outward into action. Viciously he yanked the horse around to the right and kicked it into headlong gallop, heading northeastward towards a far lowering of the ridge.

The fury in him dwindled with the wind of movement and a quietness came over him. He was aware of the horse straining under him, of its heavy breathing. He pulled it to a steady jogging.

He rode on, a short thick man on a tired horse, dirty, unshaven, dingy in old stained clothes except for the glintings of brass on the cartridge belt around his waist. He rode on, a small moving blot in the vast red-brown reaches of distance, and he passed over the far lowering of the ridge and down the long gradual slope beyond and up a wide ground swell of shifting sand and before him, stretching out of distance into distance, was the wagon trace and a third of a mile away, headed north along it, moving away from him, were seven men on horseback. The lean man on the gray horse and another man were in the lead, one on each side of the trace, bent in their saddles, studying the ground as they moved ahead, and the other five followed.

The man on the ground swell of shifting sand stopped his horse and took the rifle from its scabbard. A strange harsh chuckle sounded in the sun-hot silence and was cut short by the shot and he saw the spurt of dust beside the lean man's horse and all of them halt with sudden startled jerks and swing in their saddles to look towards him. He jammed the rifle back into its scabbard and lifted his horse rearing to wheel it around and drove it at a fast gallop back down the ground swell of sand the way he had come. He was well up the long gradual slope towards the lowering of the ridge when he looked back and saw them coming over the ground swell and lining out in full gallop behind him. Savagely he beat at the horse and it surged up and over the lowering of the ridge and as it raced down the other side towards the long level stretch to the homestead shelter he felt the first falterings in its stride, the slight warning stumblings and recoveries, and he took hold of the sack tied to the saddle horn and snapped the cord with a lurch of his weight in the saddle and let the sack fall. The horse drove on, frantic in lessening rushes of strength, and again he looked back. They were coming steadily, no closer than before, coming with steady intensity of purpose. He saw them pull sliding to a bunched brief stop by the sack and one swing down and grab it and shake out the contents in a flurry of flour and in the stopping he increased his lead. The shelter was just ahead now and he yanked the horse to a skidding stop in front of it and whipped the revolver from the holster at his side and fired two shots towards the doorway, low, into the doorstep. He caught a flashing glimpse of the little girl inside shrinking back from the roar of the shots and he was beating the horse forward again, past the corral, across the shallow-plowed strip, angling back towards the high ridge.

He reached the base and started up and the horse, faltering often now, labored into the climb. It stopped, legs braced and quivering, ribs heaving, a bloody froth bubbling in its nostrils. He pivoted to the right in the saddle and looked back. Riderless horses stood in front of the shelter and the lean man in the buckskin shirt near them directing the others. One man ran towards the closest brackish pool in the almost dry stream bed with a bucket in his hand. Another strode towards the corral with the team harness over his shoulder. Another heaved at the tongue of the old wagon to swing it out from the side wall of the shelter. And yet another mounted one of the saddled horses and swung off southeastward.

The man on the ridge slope checked each in the one swift sliding glance and stared intently at the blank walls of the shelter as if trying to force vision through them. Suddenly, as thought and bodily awareness coincided, he pivoted around and to the left in the saddle. Two of them had not stopped by the shelter, had galloped on past and swept in a wide arc towards him. They were little more than three hundred yards away. One of them was still approaching and the other had stopped and was raising a rifle to his shoulder. The man on the ridge yanked upward on his reins trying to lift the horse into motion and even before he heard the shot he felt the horse leap shuddering and its forelegs doubled under and he jumped free as it collapsed forward and sideways on the slope. He leaned down and jerked the rifle free and crouched behind the still quivering body of the horse and sent a single shot crashing down towards the level and saw the two men circle back to a safer distance and turn their horses sideways towards him and dismount to stand behind them with the barrels of rifles resting over the saddles.

He reached with one hand into the pocket of his old shirt and with fumbling fingers counted the rifle bullets there. He turned his head to study the slope rising behind him. Bare rock climbed with scant crevices and small pockets of dirt where a few scraggly bushes clung. Fifty feet higher the slope leveled in a small ledge that had caught several large stones in age-gone descent. At intervals above were other small ledges. He looked back over the body of the horse and sent another shot crashing down and leaped up crouching and scrambled towards the first ledge above and a barrage of shots battered from the two men below and out and a bullet smashed into his left shoulder and spun him falling and he rolled back behind the body of the horse and hitched himself around to hold the rifle with his right hand over it. The sun beat clean and hot upon him and the two men below and out watched over their saddles and he lay quiet watching them.

Down and across the level expanse the lean man in the buckskin shirt stepped out from the doorway of the shelter and around the corner for a clear view of the ridge and the body of the horse, small at the distance yet distinct against the rock. His eyes narrowed as he peered intently and he made out the dull dirtied deadliness of the rifle barrel pointing over the body. He walked to the tall gray horse ground-reined in front of the shelter and took his rifle from its saddle scabbard. Quietly, paying no attention to the harnessing of the draft horses to the old wagon, he walked around the other side of the shelter and started back towards the ridge directly behind. He came on tracks, hoofprints in the loose dirt heading southwestward into distance towards the far lowering of the ridge. He stopped and looked down at these a long moment and moved on and came to the base of the ridge and climbed until he was almost parallel on it to the man behind the body of the horse not quite a half mile away. He lay flat on a slight leveling of the slope and adjusted the sights on his rifle and pushed the barrel out in front of him and settled into position and waited. Several shots came from the two men out on the level expanse and the man behind the body of the horse hunched himself forward and up to reply to them and the man in the buckskin shirt tightened his finger on his trigger in a slow steady squeeze. He saw the man behind the body of the horse jerk convulsively and try to rise and fall forward over the body of the horse and lie still. He saw the two men out on the level mount and start towards the ridge. Quietly he stood up and walked back towards the shelter.

The wagon was ready. Two of the saddled horses were tied behind it and a blanket had been rigged over the wagon body for shade. Under it lay the still forms of the man and the woman from inside the shelter. The little girl, small and shrinking and silent, sat on the seat between two of the other men.

"Take it easy but aimin' for time," the man in the buckskin shirt said. "Hit for the trace then towards town. Maybe the doc'll meet you part way."

The draft team, fresh and strong, leaned into the harness and the tugs tightened and the wagon moved away. The man in the buckskin shirt turned to watch the two men who had ridden to the ridge approach leading their horses. An old battered saddle and a bridle hung bouncing from the saddle horn of one of the horses. The body of a man, short and thick with a brass-studded cartridge belt around its waist, hung limply over the saddle of the other horse.

"Did you get it?" said the man in the buckskin shirt.

"Yes," said one of the men. "In the saddle bag there."

The man in the buckskin shirt stepped forward and bent to slip a shoulder close against the saddle up under the body of the man in the brass-studded belt and lifted it away and went and heaved it over the saddle of the tall gray horse. He stepped into the shelter and came out carrying a spade in one hand. He took the reins of the tall gray horse with the other hand and led it away. Head low, staring at the ground before him, he led it, past the corral, across the almost dry stream bed, and stopped at last by the straggling row of stunted cottonwoods. He looked up. The other men had followed him.

"Don't be a fool," one of the other men said. "Drag him out somewheres and let the buzzards and coyotes have him. He wasn't no more'n an animal himself."

"No," the man in the buckskin shirt said. He looked back past the shelter, on into the vast empty distance where the trail of a tired horse led northeastward towards the far lowering of the ridge and returned. "He was a murderin' thievin' son-of-a-bitch. But he was a man." Quietly, bending to the hot task in the clean sun, the man in the buckskin shirt struck the spade into the red-brown earth.

About the Author

JACK SCHAEFER was born in 1907 in Cleveland, Ohio, to parents who were avid readers. After studying Greek and Latin classics at Oberlin College, he did graduate work in English literature at Columbia University, then embarked upon a career in journalism that took him to New Haven, Baltimore, and Norfolk, Virginia.

His first novel, *Shane*, was published by Houghton Mifflin in 1949 after appearing as a serial in *Argosy* a few years previously. A remarkably strong first novel, *Shane* has appeared in more than seventy editions and thirty foreign languages. The famous book became a famous film in 1953.

Over the next decade Jack Schaefer wrote many short stories and several short novels, including *First Blood* (1953), *The Canyon* (1953), *The Kean Land* (1959), and *Old Ramon* (1960, for young readers). He also wrote two longer works, *Company of Cowards* (1957), which some critics consider his most underrated novel, and *Monte Walsh* (1963), in which Schaefer threaded together several related stories of a working cowboy into a brilliant novelistic narrative. Many of Schaefer's books have been filmed as major motion pictures.

Today, Jack Schaefer is retired from writing, and he and his wife live in Santa Fe, New Mexico.